I0653113

Antioch, TN 37013

ISBN: 978-0-578-38931-8

Published by William "Deek" Harris, Antioch, TN 37013

Printed in the U.S.A.

William "Deek" Harris, February 2022

Cover designed by Thomas Adams

Acknowledgement

I would like to first thank God for my gift of storytelling. Without Him none of this would be possible. This book has been a long time coming. I dedicate this book to the memory of my loving mother Frances S. Harris. She was my all-time biggest fan and supporter. I love and miss you.

The Allures
of
Dolphin Manor

By Deek Harris

Chapter 1

Coming Home

It had been over twenty years since Brandon had been back to Silver Pointe. The trip back had been long overdue. As a child, Brandon spent every summer there with his grandparents. Over the years he had began to look forward to his summer vacations. His grandparents owned and operated a bed and breakfast that rested along the seashores of North Carolina. Their home was an old restored Confederate general's home with an eight horse stable. It was famous for the high dolphin activity that was easily seen from the rooms with the ocean view. Every morning schools of dolphins would swim near their enormous estate as if they were trained to do so. For about an hour and a half, every fifteen minutes or so one after the other, a school of five or more dolphins would appear for their repeated routine. The dolphins' daily frolicking earned the home the name "Dolphin Manor". The eight- bedroom, seven bathroom villa sat on three acres of well manicured and breathtaking landscaped grounds. The front and the sides of the estate were surrounded by a six foot coble stone wall while the back of the grounds were opened and merged with the seashore. Along the grass line just before the sand met, Brandon's grandparents had tables with

9

chairs as well as benches set out back for their patrons to sit and watch the dolphin show while having breakfast if they chose. Many times people would find themselves sitting there enjoying the view for hours after the dolphins had long gone. Between the house and the shoreline was an enormous white gazebo with two huge two person hammocks and a couple's swing hanging in the center. The area also served as the perfect romantic setting for an evening of bonding for couples. There were so many marriage proposals accepted on that swing that it was unofficially named the S.O.U.L. which was short for, "Swing of Undeniable Love".

Brandon pulled into the gate and drove down the long winding unpaved driveway. As his Bonneville bounced and rocked, hidden memories of running barefoot up and down the same passageway entered his mind. "Wow it looks kind of like something you would see on a postcard." his daughter Sydney exclaimed with a smile brighter than the sun that was reflecting off of the ocean in the background. Sydney had heard many stories that her dad had told her of spending time there as a child. "I can't believe grandma and grandpa didn't want to stay here! Then you would've been born here and the chances are that I too would've been born here and…" was the last thing Brandon heard before drifting off into the past. Alert and fully aware of where he was and what he was doing, Brandon's subconscious drifted to when he was ten years old. He was a skinny dark skinned kid from the Bronx and down south visiting for the summer. He remembered hating to come because he was going to miss Billy President's birthday party. Billy's mother had gotten a DJ and a permit to block the street off for a few hours for his party. Shelly Koonce was going to be there and Brandon was crazy about her. It wouldn't have been so bad if he could've just left after the party instead of the day before it. It was all the neighborhood was talking about. "Billy President's Birthday Block Party" was all Brandon heard. Brandon and Billy had been best friends since they were six years old. Brandon and Billy were two of the few kids in the neighborhood that had both parents in the house. Billy's parents both had good jobs but terrible credit so they were forced to stay in the projects just as Brandon's parents were forced. Billy's parents were so proud of him doing so well in school and not following his older brother Jerrod which ended up in prison doing life at the age of seventeen. They were going all out for Billy and Brandon didn't want to miss the celebration.

As Brandon was pulling up to the house he quickly returned to reality without missing a beat. He turned the car off and looked directly at the house and said to Sydney,

"This is it. This is where grandma and grandpa used to ship me off to when I was about your age." Brandon's face then lit up much like Sydney's, displaying their undeniable resemblance of one another. Just then the door to the house flew open and a tall dark skinned, older, slender man slowly walked out onto the porch. His completely grey short hair on his head matched his grey goatee. Dressed in a navy blue t-shirt and old worn out jean overalls filled with dirt stains, it was obvious that he had been somewhere working pretty hard. His high cheek bones and large lips were a clear give away that he was the uncle that Brandon had told Sydney about countless times at the dinner table. He stood at the edge of the porch and yelled out to them "Git yo ass out that there car boy and come pull my finger! I ain't had a good fart since you gradunated from high schools." Sydney turned to Brandon and said "That must be Uncle Tony!" Brandon answered laughing so hard he could hardly speak to tell her "The one and only!" They got out of the car and Sydney took off running to greet Uncle Tony. "The last time I saw you, you were two cent shorter than a nickel. Come give these old bones a good rattling gal." Tony demanded with his arms stretched out to receive his adoring great niece. "How was yo furst trip down south?" he continued as he put his arm around Sydney to walk her into the house. Just before they entered the house he looked back at Brandon unloading the many large bags and yelled out "I would send Carl and Rusty out to help you but they went into town to pick up some things." Slowly the two disappeared into the home and left Brandon to struggle with his and Sydney's bags alone in the heat.

Uncle Tony and Sydney stood in the foyer of the large house so that she may survey the home. "So what do you think?" Tony asked as he stood with his chest out and a smile wide enough to fill a room. Sydney's mouth was wide opened and so were her eyes. She stood in shock and amazement. She spun slowly assessing the place. When she finally took a breath she said "Wooow! It's exactly how dad described it. I mean from the dark hardwood floors to the antique furniture and everything. The rugs, the vases, bookshelves, books, figurines...EVERYTHING!!! When I was a little girl I used to close my eyes when he would talk about his visits and I would try to imagine being here myself." Her eyes were lit like a child's that had just stumbled across Santa's workshop. Sydney was so engaged in her real life dream that she hadn't noticed that two more fellows had entered the room. Sydney was admiring one of the antique chairs that sat near the front window. Her dad told her many times about how his grandmother would sit and wait for him in that chair. Uncle Tony's deep gravelly voice broke her concentration. "I want you to meet someone darling. This here is Carl and Rusty". Sydney had heard plenty of stories of the two of them as well. She was very familiar with the story of how Uncle Tony's son Carl and her dad had gotten into a huge fight with a group of white guys and how Aunt Carol's son Rusty pulled up with a car load of friends to even the odds. The three of them made a name for themselves after that day. When they finished there wasn't a single white boy standing. Rusty never would say how he found out they were across town in trouble. He always had a way of being in the know about most any and everything that was going down in town. He knew everyone and after that day, he made sure everyone knew them. They were known as the Super Cousins. No one knew but they would call each other super hero names. Carl was Spider-Man, Brandon was Super-Man and Rusty was Bat-Man.

Sydney darted over to the two and wrapped them both up and hugged them with all of her might. "Wait. I thought you two were gone into town." she asked with a look of confusion. The look of equal confusion on their faces sent Uncle Tony into hysterical laughter. "Uncle Tony told daddy that he would send you two out to help him with the bags but you were gone." Sydney told them and turned to give Tony the evil eye. Without warning the front door opened and Brandon stood with a bag in each hand, one under each arm and a bag strapped across his shoulder. "I thought you said they were gone. You know God is looking right? You're going to mess around and not get into heaven." Brandon exclaimed jokingly with his attention directed to Tony. They all laughed as Carl and Rusty helped Brandon with their bags. "Man it sure is good to see you cuzz." Rusty said in his bone chilling deep voice he was known for. When he spoke, Sydney's eyes bucked wide open. "Wow! You have a deep voice." she said before she even realized it. "I mean…" she began to explain. "If you think that's something wait until his big ass goes to sleep. It sounds like two bears fighting in a Volkswagen! I think it got something to do with him being light skinned like his daddy too. I kept telling Carol that boy didn't finish cooking in her oven. He needed bout another two or three months." Uncle Tony intervened to release the tension of Sydney's obvious embarrassment. Rusty was six foot five and two hundred sixty five pounds of muscle. After three years of playing basketball at North Carolina A&T State University, Rusty moved to Italy to play ball. He played for two more years before his career was ended due to a knee injury in a playoff game two weeks after signing a two year contract with the L.A. Lakers. Rusty and everyone that ever met or knew Uncle Tony knew he was a clown and expected nothing less of him. Rusty like most everyone else let it roll off of his back and laugh along with or at Uncle Tony in most cases. "I ain't lying though. Look at him. Him and his daddy the only two in the family that look like cake batter!" Uncle Tony continued and put his arm around Sydney and led her into the kitchen with him. "Speaking of cake, you like cake baby? My sweetie baked me a pineapple cake yesaday knowing damn well I can't eat it. I saved it for you and ya daddy. I wouldn't let Frick and Frack in there cut it. I know it's good too." The two of them slowly disappeared into the back while the three cousins stood laughing. "Your damn daddy hasn't changed a bit." Brandon told Carl. "I see I'm going to have to do some serious deprogramming with Sydney when we get back to New York. Uncle Tony is going to have my baby caring a pocket knife threatening to cut people if I'm not careful."

Chapter 2
Back Down Memory Lane

After lunch and numerous stories of when Brandon used to come down south for the summer as a kid he excused himself from the table they all shared outside in the back of the house. "Well I'm going to head upstairs and finish unpacking Sydney and my things before it gets much later. I want to take her for a ride around town and show her some of the old hangouts." Brandon said standing and removing his empty plate from the table. "You go ahead and do that. I'm going take Sydney out to the waters. Poor child ain't never seen a beach. I can't wait for her to stick her foots in." Uncle Tony proudly boasted. Sydney stood and grabbed both her plate and Uncle Tony's and said "Uncle Tony I've been to the beach lots of times. My dad has taken me to Coney Island plenty of times." Uncle Tony's face frowned up and he looked at the three fellows which were looking back at him because they knew he was about to say something. Uncle Tony stood and said "No baby, Uncle Tony's going to take you to a real beach. A beach you don't have to worry about stepping on no crack pipes or getting stuck by no hypo-thermical needles that'll give ya AIDS or some shit!" Although Carl was doubled over in laughter at his father he attempted to correct him. With tears in his eyes Carl said "Pop it's not hypo... You know what? Never mind. It's nothing!" The look on Uncle Tony's face when Carl began to speak said it all. "Ya damn right it's nothing. Best watch it!" Uncle Tony barked at Carl with a look of "I wish you would try and correct me..." on his face. He knew himself that he had mispronounced that and many words but was not about to allow Carl to embarrass him in front of Sydney. With his eyes still fixated on Carl, Uncle Tony stood and placed his arm around Sydney's shoulder and said "Baby set them down. Carl's going to take those in for us. Now come on and let's go find us some seashells before I slap a birth mark on that boy!" Sydney placed the dishes back down and put her arm around uncle Tony's waist and snickered at Carl's scolding. She found it amusing to see an adult finally getting reprimanded. "Yes sir" she said in her sweetest voice. As the two slowly walked off Brandon instructed "Don't get too far. I will be ready to go soon." Sydney never noticed Uncle Tony raising his hand above his head to give her dad the finger because he never broke his stride nor looked back. The three cousins just stood and shook their heads at Uncle Tony's expected antics.

Brandon was almost finished unpacking their clothes when he came across an old memory that nearly floored him where he stood. The mere sight instantly threw him back to a time when he was a young pre-teen visiting for the summer. Before he realized it his eyes were closed and he was eleven again. He could see himself sitting in the same driveway that he just came up only a couple of hours prior to drifting away. He was sitting in the backseat of his dad's Cadillac with his father in the driver's seat and his mother in the passenger seat. The car radio was bumping Freddie Jackson's "Rock Me Tonight" when they pulled up and turned the car off. His father was singing along as usual and was not getting out before his song went off. Normally he enjoyed listening to his father's singing but that was not one of those times. "I don't see why I have to come down here again. I hate it down here. Last year there was nothing to do here. There's no one here to hang with or anything. Grandma and Gramps kept making me clean those stables and those horses STINK!!!" young Brandon complained over his father's singing. After hearing all he could take his father belted out "Hey man! That's enough! Now my part is about to come up and you are getting on my nerves. Hush!" His father took one more look at him in the rearview mirror and sang to his wife, "When I get through loving you girl… fire and desire will burn in…" Before his dad could reach the pinnacle of his solo they were all startled by a middle aged fellow wearing a black tank top with a pair of camouflage Army pants and a bright red beret. He had crept up along the side of their car and popped up at the driver's door. "I HAD YA NOW! That's how ya had to do Charlie when we were in the jungles Saygun. Vietnam was a MOTHER!!!" he excitedly exclaimed with a smile that nearly covered his entire face. Brandon's dad was not amused even a little bit. He got out of the car steaming mad because the guy made him miss his part in the song. Also he scared him in front of his family. His father gathered his composure and barked "Damn it Freddie! You got to stop that shit man! You're going to make me hurt you! And you know damn well you ain't NEVER been to no damn Vietnam either. And if you're going to tell that lie, at least know the name of the damn place. It's Saigon, not Saygun. You nut!" Freddie could care less about what Brandon's dad was saying to him. He just kept laughing and saying "I HAD HIM!!! YES SAH… I HAD HIM…YEP!!!" while he began to walk off towards the horse stables and looking back at Brandon's father and still laughing.

By the time his dad got the bags out of the trunk of the car his mother was walking up to none other than the younger Uncle Tony with her arms stretched out to receive his welcoming arms. "Well if it ain't my favorite sister-in-law." he shouted loud enough for the world to hear. The two locked their arms around one another and Uncle Tony picked her small frame up off of the ground. He was wearing a pair of overalls much like the ones that he would wear for the next twenty years. The only difference was that his hair had not started to grey. When he put Brandon's mother down she gave him a small little jab to the chest then laughed and said "I'm your only sister-in-law you crazy man!" He took a short step back and reached in the chest pocket of his overalls and pulled out a cigarette and told her "Yeah well if you had broken my only damn cigarette, you would've been Bobby's first wife! I'm sure he'd remarry after you were gone for a couple of few years or so. I love the hell out of you but I would've had to feed a little bit of you to the fish, a little to the horses and just used the rest for fertilizer or something." The two of them laughed and giggled at Uncle Tony's quick wit. Brandon stepped from the car then started to walk to the trunk of the car to help his dad when he was called by his uncle. "Hey nephew, come over here and give me some skin!" Brandon remembered that from his last visit Uncle Tony was the one person that he enjoyed the most. He was always talking trash to people around town like he owned it. He kept a .32 revolver and a pocket knife when he went into town and most anywhere else other than around the house. His straight forward attitude reminded him of his dad but his sense of humor is what he really enjoyed. Brandon slowly walked over to greet his uncle. He could hear Uncle Tony saying to his mother "Damn Lisa what did ya'll tell the boy? You'd think he was coming to Boy's Town or something." All she could do was shake her head and say "I know. He's been dreading the trip for the past two weeks. That's all he has talked about is how booooring it is down here. I told him it would be different this time. It is going to be different this time, isn't it?" Uncle Tony smiled and placed his arm around her and said "Oh yeah. Carl will be home from visiting his mother in the morning. And you know Carol has moved here with Rusty, so he'll have them to hang with. But I can see how he might have felt that way about last year. Hell last year I was going through the divorce and all so it wasn't really a good time for me. When Priscilla moved to California it tore Carl up so I couldn't make him stay you know?" Uncle Tony's expression had begun to take a turn for the worst when Lisa wrapped her arms around him to give him another big hug. When he reached his mother and uncle he heard his father yell out to them "Where in the hell are you all going? Tony your black ass could at least grab a bag or something man." Uncle Tony placed his right arm around Lisa and his left around Brandon then turned back to look at Bobby. He laughed then said "No the hell I can't either. My clothes are already in the house. You need to try and get yours in the house. Besides you the one looking like you going to the gym with ya gym shorts and sneakers on so work it out Mr. Workout. I'll send Foxhole Freddie back out here to help you." Then Uncle Tony turned with the two under his arm and headed to the house. Brandon could hear his dad yell back "You're just mad because your big country ass is still dressing like the black My Little Buddy doll during the week and Teddy Ruxpin on Sundays damn it. And I wish like hell you would send Freddie's crazy ass back out here and I'm going to put his phony shell shocked ass IN a foxhole!"

Later on that evening Brandon was sitting on the stairs in the house that led upstairs to the guest rooms and where he was supposed to have been quietly watching television. Instead, he sat quietly midway the stairs so that he could hear without being seen. He could overhear the adults talking while they played spades in the dining room. Uncle Tony had a couple of friends over that knew his father from when they were all growing up in Silver Pointe. There were his parents along with his Uncle Tony and one other couple all downstairs having a ball listening to all of the grown up music. Uncle Tony was always the bartender and storyteller when they got together. "Hey Spoon, do you remember when we were kids the time we talked Bobby into stealing bait from John Row's tackle shop so we could go fishing?" Uncle Tony belted out after taking a sip of his beer. He sat teetering on the edge of a bar stool next to the card table everyone was surrounding. Spoon was sitting next to Bobby at the card table. He and his wife Rose were partnered against Bobby and Lisa. Spoon was Uncle Tony's best friend that grew up helping harass Bobby as a child. "Yeah and his little ass would've gotten away if he had been looking where he was going instead of right in Old Man Row's eyes." Spoon added with a roaring laugh.

"Ha ha ha! Very funny. Momma made me go back in there the next day and apologize and every fucking thing. Daddy was so mad he had to wait a whole damn week before he was calm down enough to even spank me." Bobby protested with obvious disgust still until he looked across the table to find Lisa with her head on the table and fist pounding it from laughing so hard. Even Bobby had to laugh at himself. Bobby looked up at Uncle Tony and argued "It was that damn cat. He got right under me and made me fall and bust my ass too. I dropped the bait and every damn thing. I jumped up and took the hell off running out the door. By then Old Man Row knew what was up. I ran past these two fools and they were dying laughing at me. He called daddy and told him before we could even get home. That's why I hate them bastards to this DAY!" His statement sent the entire table into hysterics. Uncle Tony laughed so hard he nearly fell off of his bar stool. Bobby caught his breath and continued "But you know those were the good old days. That's when the only people you really had to worry about were the racist white boys. Now days you have to worry about your own acting a fool too. I tell you, some of the kids in the city have no self respect let alone respect for others. This past winter Brandon lost at least two of his classmates and God only knows how many have been in some kind of trouble with the police. A lot of them don't have anyone to guide them though. That's why we are bringing him here so that he can get a chance to get away from some of the foolishness. We want him to also see where I'm from so he knows where he comes from." Brandon sat on the stairs and thought about what his father was saying and recounted the actual number of friends that he had lost and remembered two that he never told his parents about. They were already drilling him about anyone they heard him mention around the house or talking to on the phone. It was that very moment that he realized that his parents were only looking out for his own good.

While he sat thinking of how lucky he was to have parents that gave a damn, his thoughts were interrupted by "Now what do you think you are doing young man?" It was the soft and gentle toned voice of his Grandma Rose. She had eased up on him and was standing at the top of the stairwell dressed in her long night gown and housecoat. She was a small and robust statured woman but had the strength and heart of a lioness. He turned around with a quick snap of his neck to plead his case. But before he could even speak she started down the stairs and said "Oh don't worry. Come with me. We'll have us a piece of cake in the kitchen and then head back upstairs for bed. What do you say?" Brandon peeked around the stairs at his parents and said

"My folks would kill me if they knew I was down here Grandma Rose, especially my dad." She smiled and answered "Baby, you're with me. And I do the killing around here. Now let's get some cake baby." The two of them walked down through the dining room hand in hand past the card table. Grandma Rose never even looked in the direction of the table. Brandon on the other hand couldn't resist glancing over to catch his father's piercing eyes staring back at him. He could tell his dad wanted to say something but it was obvious then that Grandma Rose was truly the one that did the so-called killing. Grandma Rose was the typical grandmother but she did not take any junk from anyone. As they strolled along Brandon overheard his father tell his mother, "I sure hope we don't have to hurt that boy when he comes back to New York. Momma is going to have him spoiled rotten trying to make up for last summer." Uncle Tony chimed in with "Oh hell yeah. She has Carl so damn rotten. He thinks he can go to her whenever I tell him no. I told him don't let momma get yo damn heart snatched out of yo chest." Grandma Rose wrapped her arm around Brandon and said to him "They better leave my grandbaby alone is all I know." She smiled and they continued down the long hallway and into the kitchen leaving the others to their drinking and cards. They sat in the kitchen together and talked about nearly everything going on in Brandon's life at the time. It was the first time he had taken the time to sit and talk with her. Grandma Rose and everyone else were so preoccupied with Uncle Tony's divorce that there was little personal attention on his last visit. It was that conversation that she also apologized to Brandon for not making his stay more enjoyable. It was also then that there was an unbreakable bond developed between the two.

By the time they had finished their cake and bonding, the others had moved their little party out back to the gazebo. Grandma Rose and Brandon could hear them from the kitchen laughing and carrying on. She locked her arm around his and the two headed back upstairs. When they got to the top of the stairs she turned to Brandon and said "Wait right here. I have something I want you to have. I'll be right back." He couldn't imagine what she had for him. He watched her walk down the long hallway and enter her bedroom. Moments later she reappeared and began to head back toward Brandon. The closer she got to him he noticed she was looking at a piece of paper. She held it close to her chest and looked into Brandon's eyes and said "I got this postcard in the mail from your father almost twenty years ago. I kept it in my drawer so I could look at it every now and then. He sent it to me when he first moved to New York with your mother. I was so afraid for him that

I would pray over the card for the entire city to be kind to my baby. He was only twenty when he left." She took one more look at it then handed the card to Brandon. Her eyes were beginning to fill with tears as she offered her precious postcard. Brandon took half of a step back and said "Oh no grandma. That's yours. Dad gave that to you. Thanks but you keep it." Grandma Rose wiped her eyes with her hand and told him "I want you to take this and look at it whenever you feel homesick. It's a picture of the Bronx. There's even a clear shot of Yankee Stadium and area of your apartments. Your father circled the area of where you all stay." She held his hand and placed the card in it and told him "Put it somewhere safe in your room here so that you can imagine you are back home anytime you want." He took the card and stared at the picture with the red circle. She was right. He instantly began to imagine himself back home in the park with his friends. Brandon hugged Grandma Rose and said "Thank you Grandma Rose. You're the best!" He kissed her on the cheek and went to his room for the night.

Before he went to sleep he gazed at the postcard and flipped it over to read. The first thing he noticed was that his dad's handwriting was just as hard to read back then as it was to him then. It wasn't much but the words hit Brandon like a ton of bricks. It read "Dear Mom, we've finally gotten our place unpacked and suitable to live in. I still can hardly believe I'm a New Yorker now. I guess dreams do come true huh? I can't wait for you and pop to come up to see us. I feel like God is blessing me more and more every day. I don't remember when I've ever been so happy! Tell pop I said hello and I love you both. Your son, Bobby." Brandon laid there looking at the card all night until he fell asleep. The next morning he woke up and found it lying next to him on his pillow. He found a thumb tack and tacked it to the inside of his closet door so that every morning he could look at it. That was his way of making sure he never got homesick because he would see it every morning he got dressed. That postcard got him through a lot of sleepless nights that he stayed up trying to imagine what his friends back home were doing. Grandma Rose had a way of always knowing just what to say or do to make things all better and that postcard was the prime example. The sound of Sydney entering the room snapped Brandon back out of his youthful trip down memory lane and back to reality. "Hey what you got there?" she asked in her usual effervescent way. He turned to address her and realized a tear had begun to stream down his cheek. Quickly he wiped his face and regained his composure. "It's the postcard my grandmother gave me on my second visit here. Man I miss her." he exclaimed staring at the card. He showed her the card and the two sat down on the bed while he told her all about how and why she gave it to him.

Chapter 3

Bitter Sweet Old Acquaintances

After riding through Silver Pointe showing Sydney some of his old stomping grounds as a young northerner, Brandon pulled into Dolphin Manor to find a black Mercedes Benz parked out front. The plate on the back immediately caught his attention. There was only one person arrogant enough to have a vanity plate that read "D-ONLY1". When Sydney got out she rushed over to the car and stood in amazement at the finely engineered machine. "Wow! Now THAT'S the kind of car I want when I get older. Do you see the wheels on this thing? Daddy who's car is it? Do you know?" she asked looking like she could spontaneously combust at any moment. He shrugged his shoulders and gave her half of a smirk and said "Let's go in and see if it's who I think it is." They walked through the door and Brandon yelled "We're back. Where is everyone?" They continued walking to the back patio to find Uncle Tony, Carl and with a man that Brandon easily recognized from his visits as a child. The three of them sat at the table having what looked to be a pretty serious conversation from the scowl on Uncle Tony's face. The man he spotted was one that he could've gone the rest of his life never seeing again as far as he was concerned. That man was none other than David West, All-American asshole. He also was Silver Pointe High School's 1989 star quarterback and homecoming king. His career was cut short in his sophomore year in college when he blew his knee out in a pick-up game of basketball in the offseason. He lost his scholarship for violating team no offseason activity rules and had to drop out of Duke University. Since he was a red shirt his freshman year, he never even got to take a single snap in an official game. Every since then his arrogance and disdain towards the school's decision to drop him he got even more unbearable to even be around. He was known for getting drunk at times and flying off the handle about how he would've been in the NFL. The fact was that his knee was beyond repair and was never the same.

When Brandon approached the table David closed his briefcase and stood with his hand out for Brandon to shake. "Well if it isn't my main man Kev. How long has it been? It's been what, ten… no wait, at least…hmmm" David said before pausing and withdrawing his hand after realizing Brandon never reached back. "Let's see…Juanita and I have been married for five years and… yeah it's been right at about ten years. How have you been?" David continued. Brandon turned to Uncle Tony "Is everything ok? What is he doing here?" he asked with disgust. "MAN that's cold! Is this any way to treat an old friend and soon to be partner? We're about to damn near become family baby boy! So you can keep that cold air in New York." David boldly stated before walking away. "Don't bother seeing me out. I can let myself out just like I will soon be letting myself in." he added as he arrogantly laughed and walked out. They all watched David as he strutted out in his tailored made suit and egotistical manner. Brandon then turned to both Carl and Tony looking just as confused as Sydney. Brandon then turned to Sydney and before he could say a word like an actress on cue she said "I know… I know… Go upstairs so you all can talk." She turned and headed muttering under her breath "Man I never get to sit in on the good stuff." Uncle Tony then stood and said "Wait up baby girl. We can get Freddie's crazy ass to saddle up Biscuit and let you ride him on the shores for a little while. He needs some exercise and I need some too." She spun around with both her mouth and eyes wide open. As Uncle Tony was heading out behind Sydney, Brandon tugged at his arm. "Whoa we need to talk. You can take her riding another time." Brandon demanded in a semi bold tone. Uncle Tony chuckled and said "Boy I never knew you wanted to be called Lefty." Brandon looked puzzled and asked "Why would I want to be called Lefty Uncle Tony?" Uncle Tony smiled and looked down at Brandon's hand and responded "You must want to because if you don't let me go, I'm going to cut this right hand of yours off." Brandon shamefully and wisely released Uncle Tony because he knew Tony carried a pocket knife. Even though Brandon knew that Uncle Tony would've never hurt him, he wasn't taking any chances. "Now I'm going to take my niece to ride Biscuit. While I'm gone Carl will answer anything that I could answer. It's time the two of you talk anyway. I've done all of the talking about this that I'm going to do today." Uncle Tony responded as his tone gradually grew more agitated. Brandon released Tony's arm and said "I'm sorry Unc. I didn't mean anything by it." Tony turned to him and placed his hand on Brandon's face and told in as soft of a tone as his deep raspy voice would allow "I know you didn't. That's the only reason why you still have both of your hands right now." Then he turned and started heading back towards Sydney whom was already standing in the doorway excitedly waiting. She held the door for him as he looked back towards the stables yelling out "Freddie are you out there? We're on our way out there and yo crazy ass better not be out there hiding talking about no damn Charlie either. If you scare this child you gonna wish you was in some Vietnam or somewhere!" The two of them walked off and left Carl and Brandon alone to talk.

With Uncle Tony and Sydney gone Brandon took advantage of the time to interrogate Carl to find out just what was going on. He turned to Carl and said "Well, I'm waiting. Do you mind telling me what in the hell was David's funky ass doing here? And what does he mean since he and Juanita have been married? Why didn't anyone tell me she was married and to HIS ass of all people? Talk to me Carl. You're my cousin man. What in the hell is going on around here?" His face was full of anger and disappointment at his lack of knowledge. Carl hung his head in shame and started "Look cousin, I know I should've told you but we all know how much you cared for Juanita. The fact is after you lost Angela, we didn't feel like you needed that added pain. Man you loved her more than anything in this world or the next. The last thing you needed was to know that Juanita was with David's bum ass! For what it's worth cousin, I apologize. I have been dreading this day for the past month or so every since I knew daddy was going to call you down here." Carl slowly walked over to Brandon and placed his hand on Brandon's shoulder. "Listen, that's the least of our problems. I think

THE ALLURES OF DOLPHIN MANOR

you need to have a seat for this." Brandon's head whipped around to Carl. "What do you mean?" he asked with a look of disbelief that there could be anything much worse than what he just heard. Carl took a seat and pointed to the chair next to him for Brandon to take. Brandon took his seat and noticed that tears were beginning to fill Carl's eyes. "Hey what's wrong?" Brandon asked. He had always known Carl to be a rock and to show very little emotion so he knew whatever it was, it had to be serious. "Talk to me man!" Brandon demanded. Carl slowly held his head up and said barely in a tear filled whisper "Daddy is dying!" The tears poured from Carl after that and were followed by deep sobbing. "The doctors say if he doesn't have a kidney transplant soon he won't make it to see Christmas. You know I already gave him one of mine Kev. I don't have another to give. The doctor says his body has gotten too weak to function on just one kidney. Rusty has offered to give him one of his but after running the test he wasn't a good candidate." Carl continued through his tears and weeping. Without a second thought Brandon responded "Say no more cousin! Get the doctors on the phone and let them know I will do it." He put his arms around Carl and held him while he cried for a few more seconds. He then gathered himself and wiped his eyes. He looked up at Brandon and said "I knew I could count on you. You know how daddy is. He was not going to ask you himself. He has already been talking crazy and saying how he shouldn't have let me waste my kidney just for him to end up dying anyway. You know, just talking crazy. But I don't give a damn. I'd do it all over again a hundred times if it didn't give him but thirty minutes of life. He's all I have man! I'm sorry I waited for you to get all the way down here before I told you but this wasn't something you just ask a person over the phone. Ya know?" Brandon looked out at the ocean and before he knew it he found himself bawling just as hard as Carl did. Carl placed his hand on Brandon's shoulder. "Man listen, as much as daddy and I would love for you to do this, please don't feel obligated. We would understand if you said no." Brandon looked at Carl and said "There is no way in HELL I would deny my family a chance at life. I'm just thinking about the fact that I only wish I had a chance to save my own mother and father from that drunk driver. Do you really think I would sit back and watch my father's only brother sit and die when I could possibly save his life? I know Uncle Tony would do it for me just as my father would have done it for you or anyone in our family for that matter. Because that's what we are Carl, family!" Just then Sydney came running onto the patio telling them about her plans with Uncle Tony. The two of them dried their eyes before she noticed their tears and they sat to listen to her exciting agenda.

Chapter 4
Reality check

The next day Brandon got up early so that he could go into town alone before Sydney awakened. He had to try and find Juanita regardless to whom she was married. He was determined to lay his eyes on her without anyone trying to talk him out of it. It had been years since he had been back to Silver Pointe let alone seen Juanita but his determination was too strong to let that stop him. Brandon was notorious for being headstrong once his mind was made up. Without a clue as to where he may find her he went to the one place he remembered she enjoyed the most when they were younger. He went to the cliffs. That's where she would go whenever she needed to be alone or just to escape the arguing and fighting she would have to endure from her parents. Her dad was an abusive alcoholic and her mother was always trying to make like he was just stressed from working so hard on the fishing boats. He would sometimes be gone for days at the time which was when they were the happiest, just the two of them. But when he would return it was back to the same old nasty attitude fueled by cheap whiskey. There had been many days and nights the two of them had sat on the cliffs and watched the waves roll in crashing against the huge rocks below. Brandon felt as though if he could just see those rocks again that somehow the ocean would tell him where he could find her. He found the very spot that they would sit and talk or not. Sometimes they would just sit there looking out at the ocean. He pulled his car over onto the side of the road and drove down to a narrow opening that was about half of a mile away from her old house. From the top of the cliff you could still see the old house standing like time had stood still. He walked out onto the rocks and stood looking at the old home hoping to be able to channel some kind of vibe telling him how to find her. He took a seat on an old familiar boulder they shared many nights waiting for the lights in her house to go out. That usually meant that either her dad had passed out drunk or left the house. Either way it was a sign that she could return home without having to hear her foul mouth father calling her mother all kinds of whores and sluts that she never could've been. She loved the bastard more than she loved herself and was far too afraid to cheat on him for fear of the beating he would issue her. For a woman to be as beautiful as Mrs. Davis was in her hay day no one in town could ever understand why she would put up with the likes of a toothless old shrimp fisherman that barely came up to the shoulders of her tall slender body. Juanita was a spitting image of the two of them but yet he would often accuse her of having Juanita with some fictitious man with no name. It was his way of convincing his drunken soul that he was justified for sleeping around on her with the real town whore, Carol Smith. She was twice his size and three times uglier. Everyone in town knew of their affair and tried to tell Mrs. Davis but she would hear nothing of the sort. It would burn Juanita up to see her around town knowing that she was her father's mistress. She was usually just as drunk as her father and held no punches when it came down to saying whatever she wanted to Juanita. She would see Juanita and say things like "Tell yo daddy when he gets home that I need to see him or I'll be by your mammie's house to get him!" Juanita tried telling her mother several times how she would speak to her and the nasty things she would say but all her mother would say was "Ooooh don't pay her no mind. You know that's the liquor talk child. She's just fooling with you and trying to ruffle ya feathers with lies. Don't nobody want Tom but me. And sometimes I wonder why I even want him!" Even with that lie coming from her lips she always managed to keep a smile on her face while telling it.

Before long the sounds of the waves beating against the rocks sent Brandon into one of his daydreaming spells. He thought back to the very first time he met Juanita. He had been coming down south for the summer for at least three years by then and was used to going off on his own. It was there on those very cliffs that he first met her. Brandon had been across town on his bicycle riding while Carl had baseball practice and Rusty was on vacation with his parents for the week. It was getting late and he was headed back to the house when he saw a girl standing on the cliff looking out into the ocean. He rode his bike down through the narrow passage. She was standing extremely close to the edge and didn't want to startle her for fear of her falling the hundreds of feet to the bottom. He stood about twenty yards away and watched her silhouetted little frame against the sunset. Her long flowing hair was blowing in the wind while she stood with her hands pressed against her face. He could tell she was crying and wasn't sure if she was thinking about jumping or what was on her mind. He yelled out to her "Excuse me. Are you ok?" with concern in his voice. She wiped her eyes and said "Just leave me alone please. I'm fine!" without even turning to see who called out to her. Confused and afraid to follow her orders he answered "I would but I'm lost and don't know how to get back to my grandmother's house. I could really use your help pointing me in the right direction. But if you jump then I'm really screwed." Slowly she turned to see who the worrisome passerby was and why he was so stubborn. It was then that he had a chance to see her face but with the sun still casting its hue behind her it was difficult to make out facial features from a distance. She stepped down from her perch and began to walk towards him. The closer she got the easier it was for him to see that she was prettier than any of the girls back in the Bronx. Her voice was like that of an angel to him. She walked up to him and said "Where does your grandmother stay?" Brandon was so captivated by her tear stained face that he found himself lost for words. "What's the matter? Cat gotcha tongue?" she asked. Quickly he snapped out of his fixation trying to keep himself from looking crazy. "No I just didn't hear you. What did you say?" he responded. Brandon was used to the girls back home but she was no New Yorker. There was an innocence about her that prevailed like sunlight through cloudy skies. She knew he heard her but played along anyway. She looked at him and with a smile she said "I asked you where your grandmother stays?" The closer she got to him she realized he looked familiar. With a warm and pleasing smile she extended her hand to Brandon and said "My name is Juanita. What's your name?" Again Brandon became shy and speechless. He was so nervous he wasn't sure if he was pitching or catching. The one thing he was sure of was that he was trapped by her beauty. She reached out with her other hand and grabbed his hand and put it in her awaiting hand then shook it. Laughing at his obvious shyness she advised "This is what you do normally when someone offers to shake your hand." Brandon began to blush and became more nervous than ever then. By the grace of God he mustered up enough courage in himself to say "Yes I know. I'm sorry. I don't know what came over me." Juanita giggled and covered her little smile with her free hand and said "Well you can let go now," pointing out the fact that he was still shaking her hand for several moments after she attempted to pull away. "Oh right, right. I'm sorry. You must think I'm pretty crazy huh?" he giggled. Juanita smiled and said "No not crazy, just different. You talk funny though. You're not from around here I know." She cocked her head to the side slightly and placed her hands on what little hips she had and said "Wait a minute. I know you. You're Carl and Rusty's cousin aren't you?" Brandon then became shocked at the fact she knew him but he didn't know her. His mouth dropped wide open and eyebrows rose. "How did you know that? I've never seen you before." She laughed and said "This is Silver Pointe not New York. Around here everyone knows everyone and when someone new comes to town everyone knows." He stood in amazement that it finally hit him that she was right, he was not in the Bronx. Confused and curious she asked "You are not really lost. So why did you stop? Are you one of the fast talking city slickers I've heard about?" Brandon then burst into laughter at her questioning him and answered "Ok you got me. I'm not lost but I'm no fast talking anything. As you can see I barely got a word out. And by the way, my name is Brandon." The two of them laughed at the fact that he did barely get his words together up until that point. "Well I guess you may be telling the truth. For a minute there I thought I was going to have to put my hand in your back and make you speak like a puppet or something." Juanita said. They laughed again and suddenly found themselves staring in one another's eyes with two of the silliest grins plastered on their little faces.

Juanita suggested they have a seat over on the cliff that he found her standing on. The teens sat and talked about everything under the sun until they realized that they had been there for hours. The sun had all but completely disappeared leaving only minutes of sunlight left. Knowing that he needed to be leaving as much as he hated to Brandon stood and said "Well I think I need to start heading home before it gets much later. My family will be worried about me if I don't get home soon. What about you? Shouldn't you be doing the same thing?" Juanita stood and said "I'm ok. Trust me no one is missing me. I do this all of the time." She turned to the shoreline and pointed "Do you see that white house way down there with the black shutters and the porch light on? That's my house there. It only takes me about twenty minutes to walk there from here. I'll be home in no time. You on the other hand have about a forty-five minute bicycle ride and yes you do need to be headed home. It gets pretty dark out here." Knowing that what she was saying was right Brandon agreed that he would began to make his way home. He said his goodbye and began to walk back to his bicycle and realized it was gone. When he looked further down the road he saw another kid on it peddling as hard as he could and looking back laughing. "Hey bring me back my cousin's bike!" he yelled at the thief. He took off running down the street and realized the culprit had gotten too big of a head start and had no chance of catching him. Confused and on the brink of panicking he stood in the middle of the street with his hands on his head with his mouth wide open. He didn't know how he was going to get home or what he was going to tell Carl when he got there. "Don't worry I know exactly who that was. Come on. I'll get my mother to give you a ride home and tomorrow you can go by his house and get Carl's bike back. I hate bullies and thieves. And that guy is both a bully and a thief. He was probably just jealous because he saw us talking. Come on, let's go." Juanita suggested with just as much disgust as Brandon had. "I expect some mess like this back home but I never would've thought it would happen down here too." Brandon said as the two of them slowly headed to Juanita's house. She stopped walking and told him "Just because you are not in the city doesn't mean that life is all peachy keen in the south either. Things down here are not much better than up north most of the time. You need to understand that people are people everywhere. Don't forget that Brandon." They then continued walking while Brandon soaked in her words of wisdom until they reached her home. Luckily for Brandon her dad wasn't home to prevent her mother from using the car to take him home when they got there. Juanita's mother pulled into the driveway of his grandparent's home and just as he was getting out Juanita told him "Tomorrow I'll come by to check on you. But tell Carl that he will find his bicycle over David's house. That's the name of the kid that was on it. I'd recognize his face anywhere with his ugly self. Ugggh I can't stand him and he knows it." Brandon nodded and said "Thanks Juanita for the info and thank you Mrs. Davis for the ride home."

The next morning Brandon and Carl both got up early together to head to David's house. Before they could get out of the yard they heard "Where are you boys off to so fast? Don't you even want breakfast?" coming from the porch. The duo stopped in their tracks when they heard the deep raspy voice because they knew exactly who was talking to them. Without even turning they both responded in unison "No sir!" and tried to walk off again. That's when they heard the steps creak and footsteps heading towards them. Again like twins they both dropped their heads simultaneously. They knew there was no getting out of the interrogation they were about to have to endure. Brandon felt a huge strong hand plop down on his left shoulder while Carl felt the other plop down on his right shoulder. The two were turned to face the music by these two huge hands as though it was hardly any effort even though they both struggled to move an inch. When they were about face they both looked up and right into the old wise eyes of Grandpa Henry. He stood over the two boys like a tar dipped statue. His face was wrinkled like a cheap linen suit and short buzz cut hair as white as snow. True to form he was the not a chip but the actual block that their fathers were chipped from except for bigger. Even with his skin as worn and facial scar on his cheek from an old bar fight he was one of the most handsome men you'd ever wanted to see for a man in his late sixties. His teeth were as white as snow and eyes just as white with pitch black pupils. He stared at the two for a moment and slowly spoke "Now I'm only going to ask you this one time. Where are we going?" The two looked at one another and then back at Grandpa Henry. Carl answered "Well what do you mean Grandpa? Brandon and I were just on our way over to my friend David's house for a little while." Grandpa Henry looked at Carl then to Brandon. Speaking to the both or whichever was the boldest to answer he asked with a scowl on his face "David West's boy David? Over there on Booker Street? So is that where Carl's wheel is? I know him. A house full of thieves! Right down to his mammy." Before he even realized what he was saying Brandon responded "How'd you know?" Grandpa smiled and answered "Son if there's one thing you'll learn around here is that not much gets past Grandpa! Ya see, this here is what I do. Now like I said WE are going. But not before I have my morning coffee and you two have your breakfast. That wheel ain't leaving town. It'll be there when we get there or else." He smiled and marched the two of them and himself back into the house for his coffee and their breakfast. On the way into the house he advised "Now your grandma has cooked a nice big breakfast and it's not going to go to waste." Just as they reached the front door he stopped the two and instructed "The same way you planned to keep this a secret from me you will NOT speak a word of this to your grandma either. I don't want her all worried over the two of you and that wheel. You hear me?" The two nodded in agreement and walked in and took their place at the breakfast table.

After breakfast was done Carl and Brandon jumped up and rushed outside to wait on Grandpa Henry. Moments later they heard the front screen door open and close. Grandpa Henry stood on the porch with his tall huge frame and stated to the boys as if he were a general "Now let's go get yo wheel!" The look in his eyes said it all, he was not happy! The three of them loaded up in his pickup truck and headed out of the yard when they heard grandma's voice calling out to them, "Henry! Wait a minute." She came out and met the trio. She walked up to the passenger side of the truck bowed her head and closed her eyes. She didn't say a word for a few seconds but when she opened her eyes she mumbled "Amen" and walked away. They pulled off and away they went to retrieve Carl's bike. Halfway out of the driveway Brandon asked "Grandpa, do you think Grandma Rose knew what was going on?" Grandpa Henry never looked at Brandon but he smiled and said "Naw son. She doesn't have the slightest idea what's going on. But what she does know is her husband of forty-eight years. Hopefully one day ya'lls wives will know you just as well." The two boys smiled and didn't say a word after that. They pulled up in front of the West's home and Grandpa Henry blew the horn for someone to come out. After the second blow the front door opened and there stood a short robust little light brown fellow with a short curly afro. He walked out onto the porch in a grey Dallas Cowboys' t-shirt and blue gym shorts and folded his arms attempting to look tough. The three got out of the truck and stepped onto the sidewalk. Grandpa Henry chuckled at the little fellow and asked "Son is your daddy home?" The boy never opened his mouth but instead stared down Carl and Brandon as though he could eat the two of them alive. "I know you heard him David West. Now answer my grandpa before I come over there and beat the curls out of your hair!" Carl demand as he himself began to huff and swell up also. Brandon looked at Carl out of the corner of his eye in shock because he had never seen that side of Carl. He couldn't believe Carl actually had it in him because he was so used to him laughing and being a clown like his dad. David's dad walked out on the porch and saw his son standing in the middle of the yard with his fists clinched and questioned "Is there something I can do for you?" Before Grandpa Henry could say anything Carl blurted out "Yeah David stole my bike from my cousin and I'm coming to get it!" and was headed into the yard. Grandpa Henry grabbed him by the arm and told him "Don't you go onto that man's property unless you've been invited." David's dad looked at his son and asked "What is he talking about? Did you take this boy's bicycle?" Without blinking an eye or hesitating David Jr. lied and said "I don't know what they are talking about daddy." His dad looked at him for a few seconds then turned back to Grandpa and said "He says he don't know what ya'll talking bout Mr. Henry. Now maybe your boy got the wrong boy!" Brandon stepped up and said "No, he took it alright and we want it back. I'd recognize him from anywhere. I saw him riding off with it myself." Grandpa Henry addressed David Sr. and said "Now if my grandson says he saw him ride off with it then that's what happened and I'm not leaving here without my boy's wheel." David Sr. looked at Jr. again and said "Now DJ if you know something about this you best let me know now or else." Again he turned and faced his father and lied by shaking his head "no" without hesitating! David Sr. turned back to the three and advised "Mr. Henry, I don't want to call your boy a liar but..." Without allowing Sr. to finish Grandpa Henry responded with "Then you best not fix yo mouth to because ifin you do I'm going to make sure you don't call another little boy one but yo own! Now I suggest you get yo boy to go get my boy's wheel and now!" It was apparent that Grandpa Henry had heard enough talking and wasn't up for hearing much more from the tone of his voice. David Jr. had just about as much talking as he could stand as well and yelled "If you want some of this then come and get some but ain't neither one of you bad enough Carl." Carl looked up at Grandpa Henry for his approval while the two David's stood in the yard waiting to see what was going to happen. "Well now you've been properly invited. But I'll go for you if you want." mumbled Grandpa Henry. Carl turned and headed towards DJ when Brandon grabbed him by the arm and stared David Jr. down and said "He took it from ME! He's mine!"

David Sr. yelled out "Now hold on there Mr. Henry!" in an attempt to make one last peace offering. What he wasn't counting on was the fact that Grandpa Henry was from the old days where if you called a man out there was no turning back. "Naw David. Your boy asked for this and this is what he is going to get. Now I've been about as nice for as long as I can be and your boy has been about as nasty as he can be." The two boys charged one another like two mad dogs. The first punch thrown and landed directly in DJ's left eye. The next was to Brandon's mouth and the blood flowed like water. Carl darted to his cousin's rescue but was stopped by Grandpa Henry. "This is a one on one. And if you get in it then it quickly goes from a simple fist fight to a gun fight. Even though I came prepared for either I'd rather it stay this way." The two young gladiators continued to rip and tear into one another until they found themselves rolling around in the yard with their family members cheering one another on. Soon they began to draw a small crowd from the West's neighbors. At first Grandpa Henry was a bit concerned that they may have to fight the neighbors as well until he realized the majority of them were cheering for Brandon. The fact was that DJ had been bullying other kids and being disrespectful to many of his neighbors that they were looking forward to someone finally oiling him up. The two boys flopped around on the ground like two fish out of water and were throwing wild haymakers at each other until Brandon landed one right in the middle of DJ's nose spraying blood everywhere. He found himself on top of David Jr. throwing punches to his face and chest like a mad man. "Give me the bike! Give... me... the... bike..." he demanded punching David in the face with each word he spat from his blood dripping mouth. DJ tried his best to block the punches but wasn't very successful. "Ok! Ok! Get off of me!" David Jr. begged. Grandpa Henry rushed over and pulled him off of David Jr. "He's had enough, son!" Grandpa Henry order but Brandon was still swinging and kicking when Grandpa Henry raised him up into the air. David Sr. stood in the middle of the yard looking dazed and pissed off. He began to yell at DJ "What the hell? You lied to me and you got your ass kicked in our own damn YARD?" He was so upset that he took his belt off and began spanking DJ in the middle of the yard for disgracing the family and lying. "Get that boy his bicycle before I let him beat yo ass some more. You got me out here defending you knowing Mr. Henry keeps his .38 with him EVERYWHERE he goes. Everybody in town knows this including YOU! And you go and steal from the one man in town crazy enough to kill ALL of us. If you don't get that boy's bike out here to this man now you better!" he screamed while continuing to wheel his belt like a slave master against DJ's backside. When he finally turned DJ loose he kicked him in the ass and headed to Grandpa Henry. He stood before the three with his head hung in shame while the entire neighborhood laughed and pointed at the defeated and beaten David Jr. While putting his belt back through the belt loops of his blue mechanic work pants David Sr. lifted his head and said "Mr. Henry I want to apologize for my boy. I can assure you nothing like this will ever happen again. I think between your boy and my belt and the whole damn neighborhood laughing at him… he's learned his lesson." By the time he was finishing up his apology DJ was coming from around the back of their home limping and crying like a baby with Carl's bike heading towards the truck. He went to lift it and put it on the back of the truck when his dad stopped him and said "Oh hell no! They didn't bring it over here and they aren't going to have to take it back. YOU will ride it all the way back to their house and walk, limp, crawl I don't care how you get back but you better make sure it gets there and you bring yo little ass HOME! I'm not through with you." He looked up at his father as though he couldn't believe it. It didn't take him long to realize that his dad wasn't playing when he gestured like he was about to remove his belt again for round two. The three fellows climbed into the truck and just as Carl was closing the door to the truck he looked back at David Jr. smiled and said "By the way, we're Steelers fans. The Cowboys are losers too!"

The roaring sound of an eighteen wheeler passing by the cliffs brought Brandon out of his daydream and back to reality. He realized he had spent enough time there and needed to be heading back to the house before someone sent out a rescue search team for him. He knew Sydney would want to go fishing from the pier like he promised. On his ride back to the house he was listening to the local radio station WDQW 103.7FM when he heard a commercial for a dentist office downtown. Normally he wouldn't have noticed but when he heard the name Dr. Juanita West he slammed on breaks and pulled to the side of the road. In a fitted rush he rambled through his glove box searching for a pen and piece of paper to jot down the phone number and address to her office. He could hardly believe what he was hearing. In some strange way he felt as though the cliffs still led him to where he could find her. "Yes. I knew you wouldn't let me down. Thank you cliffs!" he yelled to the top of his lungs. He sped up in order to hurry home so that he may keep his fishing date with Sydney. If he hurried he would have enough time to take her fishing for a few hours and get by Juanita's office before she left for the day. On the way home the radio seemed to play all of the oldie but goodies he liked. They were notorious for playing old out dated songs that the locals normally complained about but to him they were just what he needed and wanted to hear. When he pulled into the driveway he found an ambulance parked at the house. Quickly he jumped out of his car and rushed into the house to find them putting Uncle Tony onto the gurney. Sydney was crying and Carl was walking behind them as they slowly rolled him out of the house. Uncle Tony's eyes were closed but he knew he was still breathing from the way his chest was moving up and down. "What happened?" he asked Carl in a panic. Carl looked at him and answered "I don't know. Sydney went into the kitchen and found him on the floor. I woke up when I heard her screaming. When I got downstairs I found him there. That's when I called

911." Brandon rushed to Sydney's side after getting the report from Carl. The paramedics got him out to the ambulance and Carl climbed in back with him and they sped off. Brandon and Sydney jumped in the car and took off behind them following closely all the way to the hospital.

Chapter 5

The Family That Prays Together

Hours after sitting in the hospital waiting room for the doctor Carl had about all that he could take. He frantically rushed up to the nurses' station "How damn long does it take for someone to hear something around here? Is this how you treat ALL of your patients and family members? Is my father ok? Somebody needs to tell me SOMETHING!" The nurse behind the counter jumped out of her seat half scared but attempted to calm Carl. "Sir the doctor will be out as soon as he has something to report. Please try and calm down. Your father is in great hands. Now please sir, please have a seat and try to relax. Is there something we can get for you?" she asked as calmly as possible. She was clearly nervous and feeling somewhat uncomfortable considering she wasn't sure what Carl may do next. Brandon rushed from his seat next to Sydney to the nurse's rescue. He approached Carl from behind and gently placed one hand on his shoulder and the other on Carl's arm to comfort him. Unaware who Brandon was Carl jumped and snatched away at first, then hugged him and began to cry out "God please don't take my father. Please God PLEEEEASE!" Brandon then nodded to the nurse whom had visibly become moved by Carl's sobbing. Her eyes filled with tears as she covered her own mouth in an attempt to not burst into tears herself but eventually failed. Brandon stood in the middle of the waiting area embracing his torn apart cousin for several moments. Before long he too was moved to tears. By then the nurse could stand no more. She had to remove herself from the area and be relieved by a nearby co-worker as she left to gather herself. Brandon motioned for Sydney to join them in their hug when he noticed her standing just a few feet away sobbing and holding herself. She was scared and confused. She had never seen her father cry other than the day he told her that her mother was never coming home again. The three stood crying for several seconds until Brandon gathered himself and said "Hey listen, Uncle Tony would be ready to take his belt to the three of us if he knew we were out here crying over him. We have to be strong for him. He would want us to stand tall like Patrick's. If anything we need to take a moment and pray." Carl wiped his eyes and nodded in agreement. "You're right cousin. I'm sorry for breaking down like that. Do you mind doing the honor and leading the prayer? I'd feel much better if you did it than I did." Brandon nodded to show his acceptance of his duty to lead the prayer. The three of them simultaneously bowed their heads as he started "Father we stand here before You today during troubled times and ask that you hear our worried hearts. Father we ask that You enter Uncle Tony's hospital room and remove any and ALL possibilities of us not continuing to have him in our lives. We beg of You for his recovery from whatever has him at his weakest. We know You as a Healer and Provider and that Your will be done but Father we can only pray that Your will be the answer to our prayers. He is dearly needed and we again ask that You step in and heal him right now dear Lord. In Your name we pray and thank You in advance for whatever may be the outcome. In Jesus name amen."

As they opened their eyes they found themselves being observed by a rather short white man wearing scrubs. He was patiently waiting for the trio to finish and recognize his presence before he approached them. He walked up to the three and said "You must be here for Mr. Patrick. My name is Dr. Hines." Carl rushed him and asked "Is my father ok? Can we see him? What happened? Why did it take so long? Say something!" Somewhat startled he responded to Carl. "Your father is ok. He is a little weak as to be expected but he is going to be ok. He has quite a bit of fight in him to say the least but will recover fine. Mr. Patrick has suffered a mild heart attack brought on by his weakened kidneys. We are going to keep him in the hospital for a few days just to keep an eye on him. I'd feel better knowing that he is here rather than let him go back home in just a couple of days. I'm going to admit him for at least a week. Right now he is in recovery and will be in a private room shortly. Although he has been quite the pistol since coming to, I would like to ask that you not stay too long. He does need his rest, regardless to how bad he wants to leave or says he feels fine. The fact is he is in dire need of another kidney and soon or we could be looking at another heart attack and may not be as lucky, pardon me, as BLESSED the next time." Carl grabbed the much smaller doctor to hug and squeeze him. "Thank you doc. Thank you for saving my father. He is all I have." Carl continued. Brandon had to pry the two apart when he realized the doctor was looking like he was about to fall short of breath himself. "Ok Carl you can let the man go now. I'm sure he has other lives to save." Brandon suggested as he separated the two before the doctor's glasses fell completely off of his face. Carl released him and brushed the doctor off as though he had gotten dust and dirt all over him. "Sure…

sure he does. I'm sorry. Go ahead and do your doctor thing. We won't hold you up any longer." Carl said with a look of embarrassment on his face. Dr. Hines removed his half cocked glasses and cleaned his lens with his shirt tail and said "No worries. After a scare like that I'm actually about to go sit back and have a cup of coffee for now. Hopefully we can find someone soon to provide a kidney for Mr. Patrick and can get him back to his regular routine and life." Carl's face lit up and blurted out "Oh we've already found someone. My cousin Brandon here has stepped up and is offering his services. He will provide the kidney for daddy." Immediately Brandon looked at Sydney as she took two steps back from the group with her hand over her mouth. Carl took one look at her young face and knew that he had put his foot in his mouth. He turned to Brandon in shock "She didn't know?" he asked. Sydney's eyes filled with tears again as she turned and took off running down the hallway and out of the exit doors to the parking lot area. Brandon looked at Carl and said "Thanks cuzz. I was going to tell her today while we were fishing." He smirked and shook his head then headed off in a trot to explain to her.

When Brandon found Sydney she was standing outside on the breezeway with her back to him. Her arms were folded and he could tell that she was crying. He stepped out of the hospital doors and stood for a moment trying to figure what to say to her. He knew her little heart was torn from the recent discovery of her dad's decision. Slowly he walked up to her and placed his hands on her shoulders. "WHY?" she cried out aloud. "Why didn't you tell me daddy? Why?" she continued acknowledging his presence and her pain. "Syd, listen I…" he started but she pulled away from him and began to walk off. "Sydney Shanice Patrick! Stop this instant. Now I know why you're upset and I promise I was going to tell you. I left this morning and had no idea Uncle Tony was going to end up having a heart attack of course but I had every intention of discussing this with you this morning. Baby this isn't easy for me either… but he's family and all we have is us. Everything is going to be alright. You have to trust me on this. It's not going to be like before with your mother." he exclaimed as a tear rolled down his face from the painful memory. Whipping around displaying tear filled eyes she demanded "How do you know huh? How can you daddy? That's the same thing you told me about mommy. You told me then that everything was going to be ok. But it wasn't. She died daddy! She DIED and there was NOTHING you could do about that! So how do you knoooow?" Brandon rushed to her and wrapped his arms around her and held tightly next to him and said "You're right lady bug. There wasn't a thing I could do. I wish there were but there wasn't and I'm sorry." The pain in his heart grew and the tears fell. He looked deeply into her little eyes and said to her in staggered breathing from the heavy sobbing "God as my witness, I'd give ANYTHING to have her back here even if it meant giving my OWN life but you... are... right! There was nothing that I could do to save her. But I have a chance now to save Uncle Tony and I have to do it. And you are right again, I can't say that nothing will happen but what I can say is that if I don't do this then 'I' can't live with myself knowing that I could've saved my only uncle and didn't for whatever reason. All I can do is trust in God and know that whatever happens is His will. So PLEASE, I'm begging you, PLEASE trust in not me but trust in God that this is what's best. In my heart I feel that He will not allow you to lose me knowing that you need me more now than ever before. Uncle Tony needs me also and that's what family does. We help one another when we are in need. And baby... he's in need. There's no one else than can do this BUT me. So I HAVE to do this because he'd do it for me." Sydney's little eyes cried harder than they had ever cried and she threw her arms around her dad and buried her face in his body and sobbed uncontrollably because she knew there was nothing she could do to change his mind. She also knew that Uncle Tony really needed her dad as well. Slowly she peeled her face from his body and said "But what if…" and was stopped by Brandon when he calmly interrupted with "There are no what ifs just faith in God!"

On the ride back home Sydney sat in the backseat while Brandon and Carl rode up front. The car was dead silent during the ride. They pulled into the driveway and the three got out and headed to the house. Before they got to the front porch Sydney unexpectedly took off running to the beach without looking back. Brandon called out to her but she continued to run and seemed to speed up. He called out to her again only for his outcries to fall on deaf ears. He wanted to chase after her but Carl restrained him by suggesting "Let me. I'd like to speak with her if you don't mind." Brandon hesitated for a moment then gave in and extended his hand in her direction to give Carl the go ahead. He shook his head then hung it low while Carl trotted off behind Sydney. Carl reached Sydney just as she was stopping at the edge of the shore. The ocean water rushed up and onto her feet getting her shoes soaking wet but it was obvious that she could care less. Water on her shoes was the last thing on her mind at the moment. Carl didn't rush her for fear that she may take off again so he stop just shy of a ten foot radius of her space. He could hear her sobbing and allowed her a moment before speaking. Then he said "The ocean is beautiful, isn't it? I have always loved coming here as a kid and as an adult. There's something calming about it. No matter what was wrong I could always come out here and look out and allow the water to wash away the problems. Sydney I know you are scared and don't quite understand everything but I know what you're going through right now. I just want to say I'm…" Before he could finish Sydney whipped around with tears once again pouring from her eyes and said "You don't know how I feel. You CAN'T know how I feel. I lost my MOTHER in a hospital. And now he's putting himself in one and not even considering how I feel. What could you POSSIBLY know, Cousin Carl? NOTHING… Nothing at all." She turned away and Carl responded with "Babygirl I know waaaaaay more about it than I want to know. I'm sure your dad has told you that Uncle Tony was pretty much the only one that raised me much like your dad is doing right now. My mother up and left me and my father when I was eight years old. My dad told me that she had moved to Europe to pursuit a failing singing and music careers. It devastated both my dad and me not to mention my grandmother as well." Sydney turned back around and added "But she wasn't dead. At least she didn't die in some hospital like my mother did. You could at least see her again. Couldn't you?" she questioned with a sense of doubt and concern. Carl walked up to her and said "She might as well been dead. And as far as I know, she probably is dead because we haven't seen nor heard from her since I was ten. She sent letters and postcards to me almost every week the first three months. After that she went to once every three or four months until eventually they just stopped coming altogether. You see, my mother meant the world to me also just like yours did to you. So for her to walk out on us that way to me was even worse than losing her to a hospital. She left while I was in school and never even gave me as much as a hug or kiss goodbye. I came home from school and found my father sitting in the kitchen crying his eyes out. He couldn't bring himself to tell me what happened for two days. I guess he was hoping she would've changed her mind and come back home but she never did. And I guess after me constantly asking where was she he realized he couldn't keep telling me she was out of town on business any longer. We didn't receive the first letter from her for almost three weeks, not even a phone call but a letter. To this day I haven't heard her voice since the morning she left and I was on my way off to school. If I had known then that would've been the last time I was going to get to hear her voice I would've said more than a simple "See ya later!" I had no idea that I wouldn't ever see her again." Carl's eyes showed all of the years of hurt and pain that he had built up as the tears slowly trickled down his cheeks. Sydney was overwhelmed and rushed into his arms to console him. She could feel his pain and suffering. She had heard about his mother leaving but never knew the full story. She then became moved to the point of crying even harder but not for herself any longer. The two held one another while the sounds of the ocean rang out throughout the sky. Carl stroked the top of her little head and told her "So you see little cousin, Uncle Tony is all I have. Two years ago I gave him one of my own kidneys so that he may continue to go on being all that I have. Rusty has volunteered but for whatever reason he wasn't a good enough candidate and your father is our last hope. He had no idea why I called you guys here until just yesterday. While you and daddy were out riding Biscuit I told him about daddy's condition and he offered before I could even get it out good. You see little cuz, daddy is all I have left just like your dad is all that you have." Sydney was stunned by his testimony and was at a loss for words for several moments while Carl gathered himself. When she finally gathered the courage to open her mouth she asked "So it's been two years and you haven't had any problems?" Carl wiped his eyes and responded with "What do you mean?" Nervous and a little uncertain she reiterated "You know… being without both of your kidneys? You haven't had any problems or anything, have you?" Carl smiled and answered "Not one problem. I was back to my same old self before I knew it. I can't even tell the difference." Sydney smiled a smile of relief then hugged him again and said "Ok! Besides, I'm just getting to know Uncle Tony and I like him." The two of them hugged for several moments then Carl said "Thanks little cousin. Thank you for understanding. Now I'll race you back to the house so we can tell your dad that you have a change of heart." The two took off kicking up sand with Sydney in the lead as Carl wouldn't dare out run her after she just gave her blessings on the surgery.

Chapter 6
Time Doesn't go back it goes forward

After receiving Sydney's blessings and a good night's sleep, Brandon felt even better than ever. For him it meant just as much for Sydney to be comfortable with his decision as it was for his own self. The only thing he had to do was call back up to New York to advise his boss that he was going to be taking an unexpected leave of absence. With the most recent turn of events he figured why postpone the procedure when he could go ahead and handle it while he was already in town. Sydney was out of school for the summer so it was a no brainer. Brandon got up early that morning and stepped out on the patio with a hot cup of coffee and made his call into work. He explained why he wouldn't be returning within the week he had previously arranged. While finishing up his call Sydney stepped out with her normal bubbly self. She took one look around the shoreline then folded her arms with a huge smile on her face and announced "Now I could get used to this! It's so peaceful and quiet here. There are no huge buildings to block the sun, no car horns blowing or smoke filled skies. Man, when I grow up, this is where I see myself. It's like Uncle Tony said, the only thing you have to worry about is stepping on are the seashells barefoot. I love this place." Brandon stood and wrapped his arms around his little dreamer then asked "So you're going to just leave me in New York by myself huh? Who's going to take care of your old man while you're off living the high life?" She pulled back slightly and glared at him and said "Who said anything about leaving you? You're coming with me mister. I can have a wheelchair ramp installed to make sure you and these old bones of yours can get in and out." Carl stepped out just as the two of them chuckled together and hugged again. "Hey what did I miss?" Carl jokingly asked with his arms spread. Brandon took one look at Carl and burst out in even harder laughter then said "Apparently the lotion bottle with those ashy ankles of yours. It looks like you have been standing in a pile of flour." Even Carl had to laugh at himself when he took a look down. "That's cold cousin. I see since daddy isn't here you are taking his place as the funny man around here huh?" Carl added. Brandon was doubled over with laughter and could hardly catch his breath he was laughing so hard and barely even acknowledge Sydney's light tap on the shoulder. "Daddy that was just mean." she suggested but was laughing just as hard. "Ok… ok you're right." Brandon confessed as he tried to pull himself together. "I should've said he was doing the 'two step' in the flour" Brandon continued and couldn't help for laughing even harder as he entered the house and brushing past Carl to get through the door.

Walking through the kitchen and entering the living room area Brandon heard a loud knocking at the front door that quickly got his attention as well as Carl and Sydney's. Brandon stopped short of the front door to allow Carl to step up and ask in a forceful manner "Who is it?" It was obvious he like the others was a bit concerned as to who and why someone would feel the need to knock on the door with such force. Carl's question was answered with continuous beating on the door. In a heated rush Carl snatched the door open to find none other than David West himself. Hotter than a firecracker Carl scorned David by saying "Why are you out here beating like you are the police? You knew damn well if we didn't hear you then we had to be in the back as usual. Any other time yo ass would've walked around back to see if we were back there." David just smirked and looked past Carl to Brandon and said "Yeah sure Carl. But I didn't feel like getting sand in my $350 Cole Haan shoes. Once I have my way I plan on making some renovations around this place to add a little touch of class." He reached into his inside jacket pocket and pulled out some papers and offered them to Carl without taking his eyes off of Brandon. Brandon stood with his fists clinched as though he could tear into David like he did as a youngster. Brandon's glaring at David was broken by Sydney walking up to him and whispering "Isn't that the man that was here the other day daddy?" Brandon looked down at her and said "Yes. That's him. But what I don't know is why he's here." Carl snatched the papers which in turn drew David's attention away from Brandon and back to Carl. David looked at Carl with disgust. In a cold tone he mumbled through his teeth "Be careful there little man. I don't think your father would like it if he knew you were around here about to blow the deal he and I are working. Now make sure you get that down to the hospital for him. Time's ticking so he needs to let me know something and soon. You all have a good day!" David turned and let himself back out of the door slamming it behind him. Carl quickly locked the door and stood there and pounded on the door a couple of times with his fist. He refused to turn to face Brandon and Sydney even though he heard Brandon calling his name. Brandon looked at Sydney and she responded "I know... I know... but can I at least just go onto the pier instead of upstairs to the room? There's nothing to do up there!" Brandon nodded and motioned his head toward the back patio giving her the ok to do as she asked. Slowly she walked out of the house and soon was out of earshot.

Brandon took a seat on the couch and crossed his legs then said "You might as well have a seat because neither of us is leaving this room before you tell me what's going on here. Why is that snake bastard coming over here and why does he keep talking about doing shit over here like he owns the place? Talk to me man!" Carl slowly turned to face Brandon and said "Well cousin, the fact is things are not going so well right now and it looks like we may have to either sale the house or bring David's punk ass on as a partner to keep from losing everything grandma and granddaddy built here. As much as it kills us to do so, we don't see any other way. People just don't come here anymore like they used to and without tenants we don't have enough money to pay the bills. David works down at the bank where we have had to refinance the place a couple

71

of times and he's aware of our bind. So to make a long story short he's offered to give us a personal business loan to stay open with a couple of stipulations. He's willing to pay off the loan with a five percent interest clause and allow us to keep the place without his partnership. But the only thing is, if we can't pay the loan back within six months then he becomes eighty percent owner of Dolphin Manor. He then wants to convert the place into some kind of sports bar named after his wack ass. I've tried to talk some sense into daddy but you know how stubborn he can be sometimes. Even though he doesn't want to do it David has found a way to talk him into it." Brandon stood and paced the floor. When he stopped he turned to Carl and questioned "How in the hell did it get to this? Why is Uncle Tony selling out like that? This shit doesn't sound right. What is going on here? How did you two let it get to this point? I mean damn, what the fuck?" Carl stood and stepped to Brandon a little bitter and said "You wouldn't understand. You see shit is different down here cousin. Everyone doesn't have a college degree and working for some fancy accounting firm making long dollars like you. So please, spare me the whole 'I want some answers' crap. This isn't New York here if you haven't noticed. Look around Kev. Do you see any guest? Do you see anyone outside?" Carl intensely pointed out the obvious as he turned in a circle in the middle of the floor with his arms stretched out to dramatically show and prove his point. Brandon noticeably embarrassed and ashamed hung his head and stroked the back of his own neck as if to say "Why did I even open my big mouth"? Carl took one look at his slightly older and defeated cousin and explained "Look man, I'm sorry! I didn't mean to fly off of the handle that way. I had no right. It's just that things are pretty stressful right now and I didn't mean to take it out on you. You know how I get sometimes. I mean... I mean... you know. You and Rust are like my brothers man. You two are the closest things I have to brothers anyway and I would never do or say anything to hurt you. You know that right?" Brandon slowly held his head up and smirked at Carl. He responded "Man listen. You don't owe me an apology. Hell if anything I owe you one. I was way out of line questioning how you and Uncle Tony run things around here. I'm the one that was wrong." The two of them shook hands and gave up a quick hug to confirm the peace.

The rest of the morning Brandon couldn't help for thinking about what Carl said to him. Although they had apologized he still felt as though there had to be something to how Carl felt. It made him question how Carl and others looked at him. After all that he had been through with losing his wife and having to raise Sydney alone he still had to recognize the fact that he was still a little more well off financially than Carl and Uncle Tony. Not long after he and Carl had their few words Brandon took Sydney fishing like he had promised. Later that evening after dinner Brandon asked Carl to watch Sydney while he took a ride across town. While on his ride he kept thinking about how much fun it was coming down south as a kid and how he hated when he had to go back up north. He remembered counting the months off before he could return back to the beach. Things were so much more simple back then. It was a warm night so he rode with his windows rolled down so he could enjoy the warm summer night air. The fresh air was one of the things he remembered and missed most about the south. It was something he valued considering New York was always polluted with both noise and smog. After riding around town for nearly an hour and realizing there was no more he could see Brandon found himself at Anderson County Memorial Hospital parking lot. Knowing that it was well past visiting hours Brandon refused to let that stop him from seeing his favorite uncle. He went up to the floor Uncle Tony was on and got off of the elevator. As he walked the hall looking for Uncle Tony's room he heard a woman's voice saying, "Excuse me sir, may I help you?" Initially Brandon acted as though he hadn't heard a word but the request became stronger and rather louder. He stopped in his tracks and slowly turned with a look of "WHAT" plastered on his face. He was a little taken to find the same young nurse from the ER the day before staring back at him in just as much shock as he. "Is everything ok?" she asked in a much milder tone. Her concern calmed Brandon and assured him that she meant no harm. With a soften heart he responded "I'm just looking to see my uncle. I know it's after visiting hours but you don't understand. He's the backbone of our family. I don't mean to disturb him but I just need…" Before he could finish she placed her index finger over her lips to hush him and motioned for him to follow her. The two quietly proceeded down the hallway in the opposite direction. Like a spy in deep cover she whispered to him "This way. He's down here. He's in the third room from the end, room 3312. Please try not to stay too long. He still needs his rest." Brandon nodded in acceptance and slowly proceeded down the hall to Uncle Tony's room.

When he reached the door he paused for a second to prepare himself for what he may see on the other side. Slowly he opened the door to find Uncle Tony lying in bed with his eyes closed and the television on with the volume turned low. He slowly tipped toed into the room and took a seat in the chair at the foot of the bed. The monitors, the trays and everything in the room triggered one of his infamous flashbacks. Slowly he closed his eyes and put his face in his hands. A tear rolled from his right eye and instantly he was in the hospital room with his wife again. He found himself standing by her side holding her hand saying "How do you feel? Are you ok?" She looked up at him with her usual bright smile and said "I'm fine sweetie, which is more than I'm sure I can say for my house. I'm sure you and Sydney have things everywhere. I'm just ready to get out of here so I can get back to work and taking care of you two. The question is… how are the two of you?" Brandon laughed and said "We and YOUR house are fine." They both laughed at Brandon's sarcastic response to Angela's comment about the house being hers as though she was the only one that lived there. "You know what I mean silly. I know it's OUR house." she added. Brandon held her hand in his right and patted it with the left and looked down at his wedding band on top of her hand. While holding that position he drew her attention to it. "Do you see this Angela? This wedding band and your love is all I need. I bought and designed that house MYSELF just for you. So although I know we were just kidding but as far as I'm concerned… that IS your house but together WE make it OUR home. And without you there in it, that's all it ever will be is a house."She smiled and with her hand tightly clutched by Brandon's she gently pulled him downward to her and planted her lips onto his and whispered "That's why I married you. You know just how to make my heart skip a beat!" As Brandon was coming up from his kiss they heard a knock at the door from her doctor and his staff. "Hi, I'm Dr. Kidman. You must be Mr. Patrick. It's a pleasure to meet you." the doctor said with his hand out for Brandon to shake. "I know you have been informed over and over that this is a routine procedure and very common. Do you have any questions before we take her back for surgery?" the doctor added. Brandon shook his hand and said "No your staff has been quite informative and her primary care doctor has gone over the procedure with Angela and me several times." Dr. Kidman smiled and nodded his head and said with a smile "Very well then. We won't prolong this any longer and go ahead and take her now so that we can get started. You are more than welcome to stay here in her room and wait on her or you may follow us and wait in the surgery waiting area. We will be going right past there. That way you can walk with her up until we get to the double doors of the surgery area and then we would take her from there." Brandon looked into Angela's eyes and said "Yes I'd like to walk with her." The doctor smiled and nodded to his staff to have them load her onto the gurney.

Brandon clenched his hands tighter and tighter as though he didn't want to let go because he knew that would be the last time he'd see her alive. He felt resistance then heard a deep voice saying "Boy if you don't turn my damn hand loose I bet I throw this urinal full of piss in yo face." That's when he realized he wasn't holding Angela's hand any longer but it was Uncle Tony's hand. Shaking his head to clear the cobwebs and thoughts he brought himself completely back to reality. He knew he was back when Uncle Tony blurted "What the hell was you trying to do, crush my damn fangers?" As if the look on Uncle Tony's face wasn't convincing enough but the fact that he was actually holding the hospital urinal in his other hand Brandon knew Uncle Tony was dead serious. "Man if you throw that old rotten piss on me Uncle Tony I'm going to take your kidney out myself. And I'm using YOUR pocket knife to do it" Brandon responded with a laugh. Uncle Tony laughed with him and sat the urinal back down but still snatched his hand from Brandon's clutch. After a good chuckle Uncle Tony shamefully looked away and said "So Carl told you huh?" Brandon could only nod his head and say "Yes sir. He told me. You know you could've just told me yourself. You're the only uncle I have. Momma didn't have any brothers. Not to mention Unc, we're family. You can always come to me. Even with the business not doing so well I wish you had just come to me. I love you and we're all we have, right?" Uncle Tony slowly turned back to Brandon and softly said "Your daddy would be so proud of you. I know I am. Thank you, son!" A knock on the door stopped Uncle Tony just in time to prevent the obvious tears of emotions from streaming down. "What the hell?" he questioned while wiping his eyes and focusing on the room door. It was the nurse that helped Brandon sneak into the room. She peeked her head in and said "I don't mean to bother you two but your nurse will be around in a few minutes to take your vitals Mr. Patrick. You may want to leave before she gets here. She's not as lenient as I." It was obvious she hated to interrupt but necessary. "I don't give a…" Uncle Tony started with his voice raised. Brandon stopped him before he embarrassed and scared the young nurse. "Noooo Uncle Tony. I need to leave anyway. I don't want to get her in any trouble. She helped me sneak up here to see you as is. I'll be back to see you soon." Brandon intervened. "I tell you what. They better not say nothing to you or I'll snatch a birth mark off a mother…" Uncle Tony stated to the young nurse in her defense before Brandon just barely stopped him with "See… you can't be in here acting like that Unc. You have to calm down man." The nurse giggled and motioned for Brandon to show a little more urgency. The two left the room with only moments to spare before the attending nurse entered Uncle Tony's room. They knew she was there and apparently pleasing to Uncle Tony. From his room they heard him yell out "Hot damn! Now did you come in here to give me a sponge bath or am I giving you one?" Brandon could only hang his head as he entered the elevator leaving his guide standing there in stitches laughing from his uncle's antics.

Chapter 7

Playing it cool

The next day Brandon woke up to find that Carl and Sydney had already gotten up and left the house together. He found a note on the kitchen table that read "Good morning sleepy head. Cousin Carl and I are going to see Uncle Tony at the hospital. Then he is going to take me to see some of the places the two of you used to go to when you were kids. We will be back a little later. Love you, Sydney. P.S. Cousin Rusty is supposed to stop by sometime today to help you feed the horses. Have fun!" Brandon smiled and laughed to himself at how much Sydney was growing up and reminding him of her mother more and more every day. He fixed himself a pot of coffee and breakfast while he waited for Rusty to get there. After he finished his meal he got dressed and came down the stairs just as he heard a knock at the door. Figuring it had to be Rusty he opened the door without questioning or looking out to see who was there. Instead, he opened the door then turned his back and continued to button his shirt. Walking towards the kitchen he exclaimed with laughter "I was expecting you to have been here long before now boy. I should've known." Brandon was stopped in his tracks when the voice that entered said "I'm sorry but you must have us mistaken for someone else." He turned to find an attractive and well dressed young black couple standing in the doorway looking a bit confused. "My name is William and this is my girlfriend Leslie. We were just riding by and saw the sign out front and thought we'd stop in to see if there were any vacancies for the night." Brandon was noticeably embarrassed and somewhat taken aback at his mistaken identity. "I apologize. I thought you were my cousin coming to lend a hand with the horses." The couples' eyes lit up like children's at the sight of Santa on Christmas. "You have horses?" Leslie asked excitedly. "Yes... yes we do. Four to be exact. You are more than welcome to see them once we... I mean... once I get you checked in. You'll have to bear with me. I don't usually work here. This is my uncle's place and I'm the only one here now. So I need to make a call to get the rates and things so I don't over or under charge you guys. Excuse me for just a moment while I run upstairs to get my cell phone." Brandon advised while patting himself down to discover his phone was not on him. "Sure thing. We're just going to step outside and get our bags while you do that." William explained as he escorted Leslie back out of the door. Like a bolt of lightning Brandon shot upstairs to quickly grab his phone. On his way back down, he found Rusty helping the couple carry in their bags. "Oh thank God you came when you did Rust. I just tried to call Carl and his phone isn't on. He is probably in the hospital with Uncle Tony and had to turn it off. Do you know ANYTHING about the rates and what to do next?" Brandon asked frantically. Rusty and the couple laughed at Brandon's lack of knowledge and continued to enter the house. "There are forms behind the front desk for them to fill out and keys to the rooms as well cuzz. Just calm down and take a deep breath. It's going to be ok." Rusty suggested in his deep baritone voice.

Rusty got the guest checked in and showed them to their room while Brandon observed his every move like a hawk. They left the couple upstairs in their room and headed outside to where the horses were. Figuring they would want to possibly ride them, they wanted to make sure the horses were well fed and not in a bad mood. While the horses ate from their feedbags they brushed them to make sure they looked their best for the guest. "Hey Rust, tell me something. What happened around here man? Why don't they get more guests than this? I mean, I remember when I was a kid people used to come here all of the time. I don't get it." Brandon questioned with deep concern. Rusty stopped stroking his horse and turned to Brandon and said "Well cousin, the fact is, no one really knows about the place anymore. Back in the day there weren't as many fancy hotels as there are now. The choices were limited so people had to go where they could. Besides, you know how grandma used to love to cook. People would hear about her famous home cooked meals and come by just to eat sometimes. Uncle Tony damn sure can't cook like grandma!" the two of them laughed at the obvious and continued to brush the horses. Once they finished brushing the horses Rusty suggested "Hey look, I'm going to stick around for awhile at least until Carl gets back. But for now I'm going to head back up to the house to keep an eye on things. Are you coming? If not then you can finish brushing the other two while I start preparing some lunch for our guests." Brandon chuckled at the thought of Rusty getting lunch together and advised "No you go ahead. I'll stay out here and finish brushing the horses. I'll be in as soon as I finish." Rusty put his brush down and headed out of the stable and stopped short of the door. He turned to Brandon and said "You know, Carl told me what you're going to do for Uncle Tony. I wish I could do it myself or I would. But I just want to say… thanks cousin. I knew you wouldn't let him down." Brandon's smiled and said "We're family man. I'd do the same for you or anyone else in the family. You don't have to thank me. That's what family does. That's what makes us family." Rusty nodded with a smile then turned and trotted back to the house.

Brandon continued to stroke the horse's dark brown coat and couldn't help for allowing himself to drift away as he was known to do. Within minutes of Rusty leaving, Brandon was thinking about one warm summer day spent with Juanita. The two of them had been together hanging out all day long. He actually ditched Carl and Rusty so he could hang with her. They spent the better part of the morning walking on the beach together just talking about the different things they liked and didn't like. It was a perfect example of "puppy love". He told her all about living in New York while she clung to his every word. They shared things about themselves that they had never told anyone else. They grew a lot closer that day because of the things they shared. Before long they realized they had magically ended up holding hands while walking down the shore barefoot. At fifteen each, neither of them had ever had a relationship but they were sure they liked one another and a lot. On their way back towards Dolphin Manor they were greeted with grandma's call out to them from the back patio area "Brandon come here baby!" He darted up to Grandma Rose to see what she needed. "Yes grandma." he asked as he ran up to her with a smile that could light up the entire seashore. Grandma Rose smiled and stroked his young face and said "Baby won't you invite your little girlfriend up for some lunch. I've made a couple of sandwiches for the two of you. She has to be hungry after all of that walking and courting. You can run in and get them and take them out to the gazebo and eat them there." Brandon's little facial expression was priceless to Grandma Rose. Embarrassed, to no end, Brandon could only say "Grandmaaa! She's not my girlfriend. We're just friends." She looked at him and chuckled. She stroked his young flushed face again and said "If you say so dear." She then laughed and walked back into the house to show Brandon where to find their sandwiches and juice. Brandon just smiled and followed Grandma Rose without disputing another word. He came back out with a tray with two plates with a sandwich and chips on each along with a drink of Grandma Rose's famous homemade lemonade for him and Juanita. He walked out to the gazebo and called out to Juanita for her to come join him. They sat and enjoyed their lunch while looking out onto the beautiful ocean not saying a word but occasionally glancing over to one another and grinning. When their lunch was over Brandon rushed their dishes and tray back up to the house. When he returned he was a little saddened. Juanita noticed the concerned look on his face and asked "What's wrong?" Brandon sighed and responded with extreme disdain "I have to brush the horses and clean the stable. I hate it and I don't think they like me either." Juanita laughed at the pouty face he was wearing and said "It's nothing. I'll help and show you how fast it can be." She smiled at the fact that he didn't know anything about the horses and she would have a chance to teach him.

Once the two of them had finished cleaning the stable and brushing the horses they kicked back on a stack of hay in the loft to relax. It was grueling work for a city boy like Brandon but not so much for Juanita. While lying back Brandon thought after having such a nice day with Juanita and getting to know her better that he'd take a chance and ask her the biggest question of all. He turned to face her and said "Juanita, I know we've only known one another for a short time and live in separate states but there's something I have to say." Juanita immediately sat up with a look of concern on her face not sure of where he was going with his conversation she responded "Yes what is it Brandon?" With her now looking directly into his eyes his courage quickly fleeted his body and was replaced with a thousand butterflies in the pit of his stomach. Confused and unsure what to do next he sat back and just said "Oh it's nothing. I guess it slipped my mind." Juanita refusing to accept his response questioned "No it didn't. What is it Brandon? Tell me!" Recognizing her determination for the truth Brandon gave in. Propping himself up on his elbow in the pile of hay and facing her he regained courage just by looking into her eyes. The deeper he looked the braver he became. He took a deep breath and said "It's just that... I've never met anyone quite like you before. Out of all of the girls in my school and in my neighborhood none of them are even close to being like you. You're kind, smart and very pretty. The way you listen to me and hang onto every word I say makes me feel some kind of way. I mean even the way you smile at me like you're doing now makes me... well you know. It makes me feel good inside. I've never had a girlfriend before so I don't really know how to even say or ask but... can you... I mean would you... would you mind being my girl?" He had a look of uncertainty on his face that was priceless to Juanita. Flattered by his coy gesture she giggled and answered "Sure I will. I have been waiting for you to ask." Brandon's eyes lit up like a Christmas tree and grew a smile that covered half of his face. It was just what he wanted to hear to make his day complete. He was so excited he didn't know if he should pass out or shout to the world that she was now his girl. Unsure what to do next he just stared at her and said "Ok!" The two love birds were so excited they were just frozen stiff like mannequins. Slowly they leaned into one another and their lips met for the first time. "Brandon... Brandon... BRANDON..." rang throughout the stable as he was brought back to reality by Rusty's deep voice. He was standing in the doorway with the couple that had just checked in. "What's up cousin? I was calling your name for a while now. What's up with the silly grin you had on your face too?" Rusty jokingly asked as he walked up to Brandon and leaving the couple at the door out of earshot of his interrogation. "Sorry man I was in my own little world for a second there. What's up?" Brandon responded. "Well I need you in OUR world if you don't mind. They would like to go out for a ride if it's ok with you." Rusty continued to joke. Brandon laughed and planted the horse brush in Rusty's chest and said "Whatever crazy." and took off out of the stable in a hurry. "Rusty I have something I need to take care of. Tell Carl and Sydney I'll be back a little later. You folks enjoy your ride." Brandon added as he sprinted back to the house.

Chapter 8
Tough Love

After freshening up and heading out, Brandon went on a mission to find Juanita. At a red light he rustled through his glove box searching for the piece of paper he scribbled her office addressed on. Finally he found it and sped off nearly running the red light and almost broad siding the black Mercedes Benz driven by none other than David West. Blocking the crossroads the two offered one another cold stares for a moment until David finally smirked and pulled away. Fueled with disdain and contempt for David, Brandon banged both fists on his steering wheel. He pulled off even more determined to see Juanita. Moments later he was pulling into the parking lot of her office. Still fuming from his most recent encounter with her husband David he knew he would have to sit and calm himself down before he could go in and see her for the first time in years. He didn't want her to see him with his face and fists all balled up and ready to act out. He sat in his seat and closed his eyes and took deep breaths to calm himself. Soon he found himself back in the Bronx as a teenager sitting at the kitchen table with his father. He remembers his dad sitting him down only a couple of days before they were to head back down south to Silver Pointe for his annual summer vacation. It was the summer following his fight with David. The two of them were home alone while his mother was out shopping for summer clothes for him to take down south. He sat directly across from his dad so they could see one another eye to eye. His dad had heard about what happened from his grandfather. He wanted to have a man to man talk with him. Brandon didn't know what to expect when his father called him into the kitchen to have a seat. He said "Son, you know we'll be heading to your grandparents house soon right?" Brandon nodded his head and grinned. His dad continued "And you know that I know about the fight you had while you were there right?" Brandon nodded in agreement again but without the grin but more of the look of shame. He knew his dad wasn't a violent person and spoke against violence many times. Brandon started to open his mouth to attempt to explain but was stopped. His father held up his hand and halted him before he could make a sound other than to take a breath. "You know we send you to the Carolinas to get away from the violence and bullshit here in New York. If we didn't mind you fighting then hell you might as well stay here where I could at least know what's going on. Now I know you won the fight because your grandfather hasn't stopped bragging on how you beat the boy's tail." Brandon smirked a little and quickly erased it when he noticed his dad's face went from concerned to disappointed. Shifting his face back to concerned mixed with a bit of pride Brandon's dad couldn't help for smirk himself. He said "Brandon your mother and I do all that we can to expose you to something other than the projects. We want you to see a more tamed and alternative way of living so that you don't end up in prison like Billy's brother. There are plenty of options other than what you see outside of these doors. We might can't protect you from everything but we don't have to sit back and let you fall victim to society either." Looking somewhat disinterested Brandon just nodded his head and said "I know pop. Can I go now? Billy's outside waiting for me to come downstairs." Looking like a deer caught in headlights, Brandon's dad just shook his head and stood. "Go ahead son." he authorized as he grabbed his pack of cigarettes off of the kitchen counter to smoke while he wondered if he just wasted all of fifteen minutes of his life. Brandon darted out of the door as though he was completely unfazed.

Normally Brandon would just head straight for the stairway but decided he would literally press his luck with the elevator. Usually the elevator in the building was out of order and the stairs were the only option for the tenants to get up or down. To his surprise the door opened right up as though it was waiting for him. He hopped in and pressed the button for the elevator to head down. He counted down the numbers until he got to the third floor and could hear voices over the trembles of the old rickety elevator. The closer it got to the bottom he could tell it was an argument between two people. There was cursing and shouting from both parties. As the doors were opening he realized one of them was Billy and the other was a boy only a few years older than them. The other boy had his back to the elevator so Brandon was unable to see his face but he recognized the black jean jacket. It had a large patch of a King Cobra on the back which let him know the boy had to be a member of the "Cobras", a gang known for terrorizing their neighborhood. The other boy was walking up to Billy and lunged for him in a flash. The two boys fell to the floor and rolled a couple of times. By the time Brandon could get there the older boy had jumped up and took off running. He took off running after the boy but realized he was too fast and had too big of a jump to catch up with him. Brandon trotted back to Billy to find his best friend lying in a rapidly growing puddle of blood. Billy was on his back holding his stomach with both hands with a look of terror on his face. He was crying and moaning in pain but was unable to stop the blood from flowing from his two stab wounds. His tear-filled eyes looked up at Brandon and gasping for air he said "Let my momma know I tried to tell him I wasn't in a gang.

That was Jerrod, he was the one in the gang. I'm scared Brandon. I'm scared!" Brandon didn't know what to do but hold his friend and yell out "Help. Somebody help me! HELP... HELP ME SOMEBODY HELP!" Brandon's eyes were swollen with tears as he held Billy while his life slowly slipped away. Rocking and trying to comfort Billy continuously saying "It's going to be ok man." Brandon hadn't even realized Billy's eyes had closed and never to open again. For more than an hour he sat at the bottom of the lobby holding his friend even while a small crowd had formed. Many had attempted to approach the two but Brandon would have no such interference. "Where were you? Where were all of you when we needed you? WHERE WERE YOU?" he cried out. Finally Billy's mother came bursting through the crowd staggering and crying "Oh my God what has happened to my BABYYYY? WHYYYY?" She fell to her knees stroking Billy's head while Brandon relentlessly rocked back and forth with his arms clenching Billy's lifeless body. Finally he released Billy to allow her to hold onto Billy's limp blood soaked body. Brandon felt two hands on his shoulders and turned around to look up into his father's eyes. He stood then took a look at himself with blood covering his hands and clothes he said to his father "Look at what he did to my friend daddy. Look at what he did.

Why daddy? Why?" His father was unable to do anything but wrap his arms around him and say "I don't know why son. I just don't know." Brandon buried his face into his father's chest and allowed his tears to flow.

Suddenly there was a loud tapping sound that caught Brandon's attention to bring him back to reality. He held his head up from resting on the steering wheel of his car to see a man standing at his car door. He had been tapping on the passenger side window to get Brandon's attention. "Are you ok sir?" the man questioned. "Yes... yes I'm fine thanks." Brandon responded with a smile. The gentleman smiled and said "Don't worry. She's the best dentist in town. I was a little nervous my first time coming to her too. But she is really good. Trust me. And she's not bad on the eyes either, if you know what I mean. Have a good day." It was obvious the man thought Brandon was sitting in his car afraid to go in like most people are when it comes to going to see their dentist. Little did he know that Brandon wasn't there for dental work. He was just the opposite. He was more excited than anything. He got himself together and finally got out of the car and headed towards the door. Just as he was about to walk in his cell phone rang. Brandon answered his phone and said "Hello. Hold on hold on. I can hardly understand what you're saying. Calm down and stay there. I'm on my way."

Without taking another step towards the office he turned around and dashed back to his car. The minute he realized it was Carl on the phone crying he knew something wasn't right and needed to get to the hospital as soon as possible. Just as he was cranked his car and about to back out, he looked back at the door of the office. He could hardly believe his eyes. It was Juanita looking back at him. She was even more beautiful as a grown woman than she was as the young lady he last saw. It was as though she knew he was the one driving but not quite sure. With the given circumstances he had no time to get out and confirm her suspicion. He was needed at the hospital and had no time to waste, not even for her. He sped off like a bat out of hell and didn't look back.

Chapter 9
Time to step up

Brandon pulled into the hospital parking lot on two wheels then jumped out and raced straight up to Uncle Tony's room. He found Sydney standing just outside of the room with her hands covering her face and crying her little eyes out. "Syd what's wrong baby?" he questioned before he even entered the room. Before she could say anything Carl rushed out because he heard Brandon's voice. The look on his face alerted Brandon that there was something wrong. "Is everything ok? What's wrong with Uncle Tony?" Brandon asked as he was stopped from entering the room by Carl. "Wait before you go in. There's something I need to talk to you about before you go in cuzzo. Come take a little walk with me first." Carl suggested as he removed his hand from Brandon's chest. They started down the hallway to converse while Sydney stood and watched them walk away. "Man, don't come telling me he's gone, Carl." Brandon begged stopping in his tracks after he realized the potential. He refused to move any farther and stopped only a few yards away to look Carl in the eyes. Carl hung his head and said "No, not yet but we need to act fast cuz. The doctor says we need to find someone quickly because daddy is getting worse. That means we have about a week to get you tested and the operation done or we WILL lose him Brandon." Brandon looked back down the hallway at Sydney and thought about how she must be feeling. He knew that from the way she was acting that she knew it was finally coming to the moment she most feared. Her arms were folded tightly and her head was low. Even though she gave her consent to Brandon he knew she was still not comfortable with what he had to do. "Sydney knows doesn't she?" Brandon asked. Carl could only hang his head and say "Yes. She was within earshot when the doctor and I were talking. But daddy doesn't know. He has no idea that he is dying and I don't want to upset him right now. She has been very understanding about not mentioning it to him, but I know she is still concerned about you Brandon. We talked and she still gives her consent but… she's a child man! I hated to have to call you and let you know but you need to get tested as soon as possible. I have scheduled an appointment for you tomorrow afternoon with the doctor's office. They will be expecting you to be there by one o'clock. Providing that everything is ok and I'm sure it will be, the procedure will be as early as within a week." Until that moment Brandon was fixated on Sydney but whipped his head around when he realized what Carl just said. It was apparent that Brandon wasn't expecting to hear that it would be so soon. Carl's facial expression quickly turned to concern and he asked "Is everything ok?" Brandon mustard up an obviously forced smile and responded "Yes… yes of course. I just didn't expect it to be so soon. But I'm fine. Really, I am." Carl looked Brandon in the eyes with doubt then asked "Are you sure? I don't want you to feel rushed into this. We can still look into finding a donor you know?" Brandon knew that Carl was only being kind and offering him an opportunity to back out. He knew there was no time to find a donor and have a kidney that fast. "Yes man I'm fine!" Brandon responded with a more convincing tone and genuine smile. There was a look of relief on Carl's face that showed he believed in Brandon's words. Attempting to shift the focus off of himself Brandon asked "How is Uncle Tony feeling right now?" Knowing what Brandon was doing he chuckled and said "He's fine for now. The nurse just gave him a pain killer and that joker is knocked out. I really think she did it so he would quit trying to hit on her." Brandon could only smile and shake his head. "That's my damn uncle." he said. Carl bobbed and nodded his head in agreement. "Why don't you and Sydney head back to the house and relieve Rusty. I'm going to stay here for a little while longer. Rusty said he would come and sit with daddy after he runs a few errands of his own and then I'll be home. That way you can get some rest of your own" Carl suggested. Brandon started to talk but was stopped by Carl. "I'll be fine cousin. Besides, I think Sydney could use you right now more than daddy's snoring ass." Carl advised with an assuring smile and looking back down the hallway in Sydney's direction. Brandon agreed and did just as Carl suggested.

On the way back to Dolphin Manor, Brandon and Sydney had another talk about the procedure to ease her mind again. By the time they were pulling into the driveway she had calmed down and assured Brandon that she was still a little nervous but understanding all the same. The closer they got to the house Brandon realized there was another car in the yard. It wasn't the one the new guests were riding. When Sydney and he walked in the house he found Rusty standing behind the counter looking down and reading the newspaper. With excitement plastered all over his face Brandon asked "Hey who's white Cadillac is that parked outside? Don't tell me there's another guest already." Rusty never drew his attention away from his paper but answered "Yeah kinda sort of." He looked up briefly then back down to his paper and said "Won't you go out back and introduce yourself before I leave." Brandon agreed and headed for the back with Sydney following closely behind him. The two stepped out back to find a lady standing in the middle of the yard halfway to the gazebo. Her back was to the house as she looked out at the gazebo and the oceanic background. The light wind was blowing both her yellow sundress and shoulder length hair to the right of her. The closer Brandon got the more familiar she became. It was Juanita and he could hardly refrain from darting out to her. Sydney noticed the smile growing on his face and asked "Do you know her daddy?" Her words stopped him in his tracks to remind him that she was still walking with him. He tore his attention from Juanita and looked at Sydney and stated "Yes baby. She's an old friend of mine. Why don't you run back to the house and see if there's anything Rusty may need help with. I'll be there soon." Sydney's giggling brought a bigger smile to Brandon's face because he knew that meant Sydney knew there was something to his old friend and she didn't disapprove. "Uuuu daddy, you like her don't you?" she joked. Brandon's head snapped back around to Sydney as he smiled and said "What? Go somewhere." Sydney shook her head then turned and slowly skipped away.

Brandon waited for Sydney to get halfway back to the house before he continued to approach Juanita. He was less than two steps away from her when she spoke. Her voice was soft and sweet like an angel. It was as though it was trapped in the breeze when she said "I thought that was you, but I tried to tell myself that I was wrong. I didn't want to get my hopes up just to have them crushed if I were wrong. I stood at that door for nearly thirty minutes waiting to see if you were going to come back to that parking lot. I even cancelled the appointment I was about to see and all that followed. I had to ride up here to see for myself." Brandon was frozen stiff and couldn't move a muscle. Juanita slowly turned to face him so that she may have visual confirmation. The two stood admiring one another for several seconds before Brandon could open his mouth to say a word. Finally the words seemed to return to him as he said "You haven't changed a bit. Still as beautiful as the last time I saw you. How have you been?" Juanita coyly looked down and away then back to him and smiled. "You always did have a way with words. Just a charmer aren't you?" she said as she wiped away the single tear that began to trickle down her cheek. "I may be a lot of things but I'm no liar." Brandon responded with a smile as he walked even closer to her. "And I see that you are still the Rose Bud I remembered. Sensitive and delicate as ever. No crying allowed Rose Bud." he whispered as he gently wiped her tear. The two embraced one another with a strong and passionate hug. She placed her head on his chest and gasped heavily as though a huge weight was lifted from her. He stroked and caressed the back of her head while he held onto her as though she was going to blow away. "Walk with me." he requested. "Where to?" she answered. Brandon lifted her face with the tip of his finger and said "Walk with me on the beach until we run out of sand." Juanita's heart pounded so heavily he could feel it himself. "That could be a mighty long walk." she responded as she gazed into his eyes. "I know." Brandon said as he lightly smiled at her. Juanita grabbed his hand and said "Let's go." They both kicked off their shoes and started down the shore hand in hand like they used to when they were kids.

The water rushed their naked feet as they strolled along the shore in silence for several moments. Ultimately their silence was broken when Juanita said "I can't believe you remembered." Brandon smiled and questioned "What's that?" Juanita's innocent giggle was pleasing to Brandon. "What can't you believe that I remembered?" he asked again. She looked off and said "You know. The little pet name you gave me when we were kids. I can't believe you still remembered that. That's what." Brandon chuckled and said "How could I forget? How could I forget ANYTHING about you?" Juanita stopped walking when he said that. She turned to him and looked up into his eyes. "I haven't been called that or anything else in so long. Thank you for being so kind." she confessed then let go of his hand and took off running back towards the house. Brandon gave chase and quickly caught up with her. He grabbed her hand to stop her to talk. "What's wrong? What happened?" he asked with deep concern that he may have done something wrong. "Brandon I can't do this. I just can't." she pleaded with tears pouring from both eyes like waterfalls. "Do what? Is there something I did? Talk to me please." Brandon begged as she continued to bawl her eyes out. Gasping for air and her words Juanita blurted out "I can't fall in love with you again. I can't do it just for you to run off and leave me here with HIM!" Her sobbing became stronger and louder as she buried her face in his chest. Brandon wrapped his arms around her to console her. "I hate the way I feel for you Brandon. I hate not being able to live the life we said WE would one day live. Do you remember how we would plan our lives out sitting in that swing? Every year someone would check into your grandparents place and find love sitting under that gazebo. WE found love sitting under that gazebo but WE were the only ones that never had the happily ever after Brandon. WHY?" Juanita cried out. At that moment Brandon knew there were still feelings that were in both of them that never got a chance to flourish. He had no answer for her other than "I don't know why Rose Bud. I had no idea you even still had feelings for me too. Besides, you and David are married now." Juanita pulled herself away from Brandon and yelled "David!" Then she took off running and crying again with Brandon running behind her yelling "Juanita wait." That time she had no intention of being caught. She ran so hard and fast that once she got back to the yard she didn't even stop to grab her shoes. She ran straight to her car and took off leaving Brandon standing on the beach looking confused.

Chapter 10
When All else fails

That night after dinner Brandon couldn't help for thinking about everything Juanita said to him. He kept reliving every emotion from the moment they first saw one another again until the moment she took off running. He went outside and figured he'd sit out on the patio and reflect. He fixed a drink of cognac to unwind and stepped out back and took a seat. The moon was full and hung high above the ocean. The rays were bright and illuminating. It was as though its sole purpose was to shine just to put the gazebo on display. Looking closely he noticed he wasn't the only one that decided to go out back. He saw the young couple that had checked in that day sitting in the swing under the gazebo. It was obvious they were deeply in love by the way they were wrapped up in each other's arms kissing. Brandon sat back in his chair and propped his feet up on the rail surrounding the patio. As he glanced up at the bright shiny moon he found himself drifting off to the night of Juanita's senior prom. His parents had allowed him to come back down south to escort her. It was a night that he had relived over and over as though it had only just happened. The most memorable time of the entire course of the day was the time they shared under the gazebo. They had many long talks while sitting in that swing but none like that particular one. The night was so magical that he could still remember the scent of the perfume she wore. Her hair and make-up were flawless. She wore a peach colored prom dress with a strand of pearls that actually came from the very ocean they sat before. It was one of the few things she cherished most. It was a necklace her mother inherited from her grandmother. It consisted of pearls that were discovered by her grandmother's father whom was a fisherman himself. Over the years he collected the pearls from the many oysters caught in his net until he had enough to string up for his only daughter. Brandon remembered how enthralled she became while telling him the history behind the necklace and how her eyes lit up. It was also the night he told her of how the swing they shared got its name "S.O.U.L." and why it was so special to his family. After Juanita had shared such a personal story with him he felt compelled to share his.

The two of them were sitting side by side and Brandon looked her in her eyes. He stared and said "That was an amazing story about this amazing necklace. I like stories like that. It kind of reminds me of the story about S.O.U.L. My father told me about it when I was a kid but it took my grandmother to tell it to me for it to really hit home for me. You see my grandmother and grandfather never really had much other than themselves. When my grandfather got out of the military he couldn't really find much work due to an injury he suffered from the Korean War. Although he wasn't completely disabled he couldn't really do quite enough to work on any of the fishing boats like most men. His back was full of shrapnel from a hand grenade so it would give out on him from time to time. Well because he was partially disabled he drew disability from the Army but not enough to support a wife and two children. So instead of him sitting around feeling sorry for himself he had an idea to start his own business. Well there was a house for sell that had been vacant for a couple of years. It needed some repairs that were minor but there were several and no one wanted to take the time or money to repair it. The city had threatened to condemn it if the owners didn't either find a buyer or fix it themselves. When granddaddy got wind of the proposition the owners were facing he went to them with a proposition of his own. He told them that he would take the house off of their hands but only on one condition." Juanita was clinging to Brandon's every word. Her eyes were bigger than fifty cent pieces. She was excited to no end and begged him to tell her as Brandon stood to his feet. "What was it? What was it?" she pled. Knowing that he had her undivided attention Brandon continued with "Well the condition was that he cut the price down by one fourth of the asking price and that the owner left the horses that were housed in the stable out back. Considering granddaddy could never afford to buy the material nor hire the help required to fix up the old house the owner agreed. He figured why not? The city was going to tear it down soon anyway and he would be out of any chances to make anything from it so why not let this crazy black man waste his money. What the owners didn't know was granddaddy had already gone to the city and asked for a design-build contract and right-of-way agreement." Seeing that Juanita was obviously unaware of the terms Brandon added "To make a long story short. He got the government to give him money and more time to repair the house as long as it was a commercial property. That's how this house became a bed and breakfast. Granddaddy also saved money by instead of hiring fancy contractors but by doing most of the work himself along with his four other brothers. They were all fishermen but two of them would work with granddaddy while the other two would go out on the boats. They rotated days so they would all be able to continue fishing and provide for their own families. Although granddaddy paid his brothers what he could, occasionally granddaddy would hire an out of work fisherman here and there to allow his brothers to get more time in on the boats. Before long "Dolphin Manor" was finished and open for business with about three weeks to spare on the contractual agreed upon time. That's when he took on the job of building this gazebo and swing by his self. He wouldn't allow anyone to help him no matter how many times his brothers offered. This was his pride and joy. Every detail was hand carved by granddaddy and no one else was even allowed to help." Juanita's jaw dropped wide open as she took a look around the gazebo she had seen so many times as though it was her first time seeing it. Brandon continued and added as he took his seat back next to her on the large swing "Not only did he build this huge gazebo, but he also made this very swing that we are sitting in now. You see there's something special about this swing. Granddaddy put so much love and dedication in it that it seems to create love within whoever takes a seat in it. Grandma Rose says that's why when couples would come out here and sit long enough they'd eventually fall in love. If they were already in love, well their love would grow even stronger for one another. It would usually result in a marriage proposal. As far as I know, no man has ever been turned down when he asked for a lady's hand in marriage. Not only that, but people had actually sent letters back to thank grandma and granddaddy for the swing. Some even called it magical. That's when it earned its name "S.O.U.L."! It's an acronym that stands for Swing Of

Undeniable Love." Juanita's eyes slowly closed as Brandon leaned in and concluded his story with a kiss on her lips.

The sound of footsteps on the patio jarred Brandon back to reality. They were from Carl as he was coming out to check on Brandon. "I hear you had a visitor today." Carl inquired not realizing he had just interrupted one of Brandon's most memorable flashbacks of Juanita. With a look of dejection clearly plastered on Brandon's face he sighed and then responded "Yeah but I don't think she will be coming back. I think she is still upset that I didn't come back for her." Carl pulled a chair up next to Brandon and took a seat. He placed the remaining bottle of liquor on the table and poured himself a drink and topped off Brandon's. "Look cuzz…" Carl started as he paused after taking a sip of his cognac. He turned and faced Brandon so he could look him in the eyes and continued with "You take far too much credit for other people's downfalls and misfortunes. Juanita is not upset that you didn't come back. She is upset because she stayed. It was not your responsibility to save her. She is a BEAUTIFUL woman and smarter than most people period. Her only setback was fear. She like many people here were too comfortable to step out and find what they wanted in life." Brandon looked extremely confused and asked "What do you mean? She went to college didn't she? I mean she enrolled into North Carolina Central

University right? How else could she become a dentist?" Carl chuckled and added "Oh yeah, she went to NCCU but only for one year. After that year she came RIGHT back here with the rest of us. You see Juanita got her degree after David's punk ass came back and started working at the bank. She was working at the diner near the docks near her mother's house. That's when captain asshole came along with his employee loans and bullshit talk game and convinced her that he was the answer to all of her problems. He paid for her to go to school and took care of her and her mother's bills while she was in school so she didn't have to work at the diner. Then after her mother passed away she felt obligated to stay with him considering all that he had done for her. She HATES his ass. She hates this town. She hates damn near everything that has any connection to him. You see David has always been an ass and always will be an ass. After he had her where he wanted her he has held it over her head every since. He has at least two other women right here in town that he is seeing on a regular. She knows about it but tries to ignore it." Brandon's face had a look of shock for a moment. He knew that her mother was the same way when Juanita was a kid. Carl took another swig of his drink and continued "Oh yeah. That bastard has been doing her dirty and the entire town knows it. He'll get drunk and curse her out in front of anybody that's around. This one time he took her out to dinner and one of the chicks he was messing with showed up. She began to curse both David AND Juanita out. Instead of getting in her ass about being disrespectful, this sorry son of a bitch gets up and leaves both of them there. THEN he walked BACK into the restaurant and yells 'well are you coming or what?' When Juanita stood up to walk out he told her 'Not you stupid. I'm talking to her!' Needless to say the other woman walked out with him and left Juanita sitting at the table crying her eyes out." Carl sat back in his sit and knocked back the rest of his drink and said "I'm telling you cousin, that David is a piece of work. Daddy said he would've shot him in the nuts if he had been there just because. That's one nasty spirited man. So she may have wished you had come back for her but I can assure you, she is more upset at the fact that she stayed. Trust me. Judging by the look on your face, I won't tell you anymore of the horror stories. Just know that that was not even the worst. That's just a sample."

The two of them continued sitting outside drinking and reminiscing about the old days of when Brandon would come down for the summer. Even with all of the memories of the good times they had as kids Brandon still couldn't help for thinking about how David had been treating Juanita. He was so hurt to hear that she was allowing herself to become not just the woman her mother was but even worse. For years he witnessed with his own eyes how her mother was humiliated by Juanita's father. The hurt and shame they both had to endure was painful even for him. Brandon was even there with her when her father passed away. He was down for the summer when her dad died from a heart attack. After seeing how her mother was treated for so many years Brandon still found it hard to believe that she would allow herself to be in a similar situation. Before long, Brandon and Carl had almost finished the rest of the bottle and the couple that was renting the room was headed back towards the house to turn in for the evening. The two lovebirds walked up and greeted the cousins. William had his arm around his girlfriend Leslie when they walked up. They were both grinning from ear to ear when Leslie announced "I just want to say I have really enjoyed the stay here so far. I can't believe you guys are not online. This is the PERFECT get away. Not to mention William just proposed to me under the gazebo. I know you guys don't know us from Adam but I felt like I owe you a big thanks." Her eyes had started to fill up with tears as she held her hand out to show off her new engagement ring to the two. Brandon and Carl both stood and congratulated the lovers and hugged them both. "This calls for a toast before bed" Carl suggested holding up the nearly empty bottle of liquor. Leslie laughed and said "Oh no. I'm headed to the room. You boys stay and enjoy. William I'll be waiting. So don't stay out too long baby." William grinned and asked "Are you sure you don't mind baby?" Leslie stood in the door and answered in a rather sultry and inviting voice "As long as you don't make me wait too long." Brandon and Carl both looked off and away as if they were not even standing there. She blew him a kiss and disappeared into the house to await her new fiancé.

Chapter 11
All That Glitters Isn't Gold

The next morning Brandon woke up earlier than normally and walked downstairs. When he went outside to watch the waves roll in with his morning cup of coffee he found Sydney and Juanita having a conversation. "Good morning daddy." Sydney said as she stood and greeted Brandon with a kiss and a smile. Perplexed and a bit concerned Brandon responded with "Good morning cupcake. I see you've met Mrs. West." Juanita smiled and said "Yes. You have a very bright little lady here Brandon. She reminds me of a certain little New Yorker I remembered years ago." Brandon grinned as he clutched his warm cup of java with both hands. He looked at Sydney and asked "Sweetie do you mind going into the kitchen and starting on some breakfast while I speak with Mrs. West for a minute? She rolled her eyes and sighed but slowly walked off saying "Bye Mrs. West. It was nice meeting you." Brandon and Juanita both chuckled at Sydney's obvious rebellion to leaving. Juanita gave a little wave goodbye and said "The pleasure was all mine Ms. Sydney but please call me Ms. Juanita like we discussed earlier. Mrs. West is not necessary sweetie." Brandon raised one eyebrow and said "Oh really now?" Sydney smiled and retreated to the kitchen as she was instructed. Once out of sight Brandon turned to Juanita and gave her the parental stare down. "So it's Ms. Juanita huh?" he questioned with a sarcastic grin on his face. Juanita glanced down and responded "Yes but please don't be mad at me. That's part of the reason I came back. There are some things we need to talk about. First I want to apologize for the way I ran away from here yesterday. That was totally out of character and uncalled for on my behalf. You did nothing wrong and you didn't deserve that. It was way out of line and unnecessary. Please forgive me." She paused and waited for Brandon to respond. Instead of speaking he offered a mere head nod and kept silent as she continued. She walked up to Brandon and held her hand out to him and said "If you wouldn't mind, I'd like to continue the walk we started. I promise not to run off this time." Brandon looked down at her hand and back into her eyes then said "How do I know you won't sprint away again? I mean, you are wearing shorts and track shoes. Yesterday you had on a dress and ran like the wind. Today you seem to be pretty prepared for whatever." The smirk on his face eased the tension a little for her so she sheepishly withdrew her hand and said "Ok I guess I had that one coming. Now that we've both been cut can we start the healing process?" Brandon placed his cup on the table and held his hand out to show Juanita the way to the beach shore and said "After you madam." She walked off of the patio area with Brandon following closely behind her.

They walked hand in hand for about thirty minutes reminiscing about the good old days until Brandon finally stopped as they approached one of the many piers tapered along the shoreline. He looked deeply into her eyes and said "So far you have kept your word about not running off but now it's time that you tell me what it was that you wanted to talk about. What was this Ms. Juanita instead of Mrs. West thing with Sydney?" Juanita smiled and said "Do you realize where we are Brandon?" He looked around and briefly surveyed the area and cynically said "Of course I do. We're in Silver Pointe on the beach. Now what does that have to do with the price of tea in China?" She gave him a look that wiped away his sarcastic look and attitude. "Ok ok. I give up. Where are we?" he shamefully asked. Juanita spun around and asked "You really don't remember do you? Underneath that pier right over there is where you first told me that you loved me. We were so young but full of love for one another. That's also the place where we first agreed to spend the rest of our lives together. Do you remember now?" Brandon's eyes lit up like a kid with a new toy when the memories came back to him. "Yes now I remember. I was down for the summer and you came over to see me the very first day that I was here on that particular visit. How in the hell did I forget? You were at grandma's house waiting for me to arrive. Rusty and Carl were pissed because I took off with you instead of going riding around town with them." Brandon continued as he laughed at how he was beginning to remember the good old days. They held hands and walked off as Juanita said "Brandon I know you have heard about David and I being together and all but there's something I must tell you." Brandon looked a bit concerned and braced himself for what he expected to be the worst. "What is it Rose Bud? You know you can talk to me about anything." he suggested. They reached the bottom of the pier and stopped underneath the first post. "Well Brandon, the fact is...

David and I... well we've been together for awhile now and you know... he and I... how do I say this without looking and sounding hypocritical?" Juanita said while hanging her head low. Brandon placed his index finger on her chin and raised her head to look him in the eyes and asked "Is everything ok? Has he..." Before he could finish she blurted out "No he hasn't done anything. It's nothing crazy like that but... I'm sick of living a lie Brandon. He and I have been telling people that we are married for years now. The fact is we are no more married than you and I are married. We don't even sleep in the same room at the house let alone the same bed. I've been living this lonely lie of a life for so long that I don't know what else to do. Brandon he is the worst person that I've EVER known. The only reason I haven't left is because he keeps holding over my head the fact that he helped my mother and me after my father passed. For someone that is impotent and erectile challenged he is the most self centered person that I have ever met." Brandon stood in amazement as he held her hands and listened to her pour out her heart to him. "So that's why you told Sydney to call you Ms. Juanita instead of Mrs. West?" he questioned with a look of discovery on his face. Juanita lowered her head and nodded yes. Slowly she lifted her head and said "I wanted to tell you the last time I was over here but we got to talking about other things and before I realized it my heart got in the way of my words. I never really got over you Brandon. I don't know why I even put up with David but I do. I feel like a prisoner of war most of the time. Please don't hate me for the way I acted. I really am sorry." Brandon released her hands and covered his face with both hands and turned away and then back to her and said "Let me get this straight. You're trying to tell me that you and David are NOT married and the two of you aren't even intimate?" Juanita hung her head and answered "I haven't been made love to in years. We don't even kiss. The mere thought of him touching me that way sickens me." Slowly the tears began to fall and Juanita tried smothering her sobbing by covering her face. It was obvious that she had been carrying that pain around for a long time and finally got a chance to release it. Brandon took her into his arms to comfort her hoping she would stop crying but it only seemed to force more tears from her.

After several moments of bawling she lifted her head from his tear soaked shirt and said "I am SO sorry for unloading on you that way. We were having such a wonderful time and I ruined it with pouring out all of my problems onto you, literally." she added and pointing out the wet spots on Brandon's shirt from her tears. He looked down at his shirt with a smirk and said "Don't worry about it. I know the feeling all too well. Trust me." Wiping the tears from her eyes Juanita asked "How so? I'm sure you have plenty of women just THROWING their selves at you back in New York." Brandon smiled then looked off and said "You're giving me far too much credit. After my wife passed away I've only entertained two women, and entertained only." Juanita cocked her head to the side then looked at Brandon out of the corner of her eye and said "Now Brandon, you can come clean with me. I mean it's me you're talking to here. I know damn well you have been with more than just TWO women over the years. I mean really now?" Brandon laughed and said "Now what is that supposed to mean?" Juanita gave a little chuckle then stepped back to assess Brandon as though he were up for sale. She looked him up and down then said "Boy please! Look at you. You're six feet plus of chocolate dream with a smile that would make a nun blush. Gone somewhere with the lies you tell. I mean really now? You want me to believe that a single man with ALL of THAT is walking around New York and not ONE sister has tried to snatch you up? I may be a crazy but I'm no fool Brandon." Brandon blushed and smiled at her mannish behavior and mocking performance as she strutted and circled him as though she was a pimp from the seventies. Brandon couldn't help for falling out laughing at her comedic

119

conduct. With one eyebrow cocked and half of a smile he told her "You need to stop it. You are killing me. Besides, I have enough on my plate with trying to raise Sydney and working. I don't have any time to date and I refuse to run women in and out of her life trying to find Ms. Right or Ms. Right Now! I mean I've had a few women to approach but when they realize that I don't have the time to give them that they are seeking they tend to fall back. Sydney and I are all we have and I will NOT allow that to be broken for the sake of some woman that can't understand that. So for now, I've chosen to be single. Maybe one day I will find a woman that can understand that I'm a package deal and not some horny old man that puts his hormones first." Juanita smiled and nodded her head to show her approval of every word she heard from him.

She reached for his hands and he accepted them both as they looked deeply into each other's eyes. She could not help for asking "Brandon, I hope I'm not being too personal but I have to ask. What happened to your wife?" Brandon slowly released her hands and turned away from her and lowered his head. Apprehensively she gradually walked up behind him and said "I'm sorry. I didn't mean to..." Before she could complete her apology Brandon spoke "She died in surgery. It was supposed to have been a routine procedure, or at least that's what the doctors said it was going to be. I guess they forgot to tell us that she may have an allergic reaction to the anesthesia and she could have a seizure right there on the operating table. She went in to have a tumor removed from her breast which was located close to her heart. But instead they butchered my wife like some lab monkey." He turned to face Juanita with a single tear trickling down from his left eye and a smug expression on his face when he mocked the surgeon that came to explain to him what happened to his wife "We had no idea that her body would react this way to the medication. We did all that we could Mr. Patrick but we lost her." Brandon looked off into the sky to attempt to hold back the tears but was unsuccessful. They began to pour down like a shower as he continued "I mean he was as nonchalant as though he was talking about he lost a game of basketball or some shit. I was so devastated at how matter of fact he was that I lost it when he tried to just walk off without further explanation. By the time they pulled me off of him I was covered in his blood from punching him in the face so many times that I didn't know where I was anymore. I mean he came out and just said it to me like she was some kind of stray dog from the street. I couldn't handle it so I lost it. Eventually after going through a long drawn out lawsuit I discovered that he severed her artery while she was having her seizure and was at fault. That was why the bastard was trying to brush it off as though she just happened to have an allergic reaction. One of the assisting nurses in the surgery came forth and admitted to attempt to tell him that he was getting too close. He allowed his ego to cost him his practice and a broken nose but none of that brought my wife back. She still never made it out of that fucking operating room alive. While his ass may have lost everything he had, he still got to go home to his family at the end of the day. He could've just said it was an accident and possibly gotten away with it but because he did such a poor job at repairing the artery and the fact that other staff members that participated in the surgery spoke up against him he is no longer allowed to practice medicine in the US ever again."

Juanita was moved by Brandon's story to point she began to shed tears from his sincere love for his belated wife. She wrapped her arms around his waist and held him tightly. "I can tell you are still hurting" she said with her face buried in his chest. "Poor Sydney without her mother and you left to raise her all by yourself. I commend you Brandon for doing such a great job with her. She is a lovely young lady and I'm sure your wife is looking down on the two of you with a smile." she continued. Brandon held Juanita back and said "Yes she is. I can feel Angela's presence sometimes through Sydney. I miss her so much but its Sydney that helps me get through each day. Syd is really concerned about me going through this kidney transplant with Uncle Tony. She feels that she is going to lose me the way she lost her mother." Juanita's facial expression changed as though she had seen a ghost. "What transplant?" she asked with concern. All of a sudden it hit Brandon that they hadn't discussed the operation. With a smile to comfort Juanita's concern Brandon explained "Yes that's the reason Carl and Uncle Tony asked me to come here. Uncle Tony is not doing very well. He is need of a kidney and as it looks I'm probably the only one that can save him. As a matter of fact I should be heading back now. I have a doctor's appointment shortly to see if I am going to be able to even donate mine and that there are no issues. I can't see why there would be but I guess its all routine." On the way back to the house Brandon explained to Juanita everything that had happened within the past few days of his arriving back in Silver Pointe. By the time they reached the house Juanita was nearly in tears again. The two stopped just shy of the patio when Brandon noticed Juanita's tears. He turned and wiped her tears away with the knuckle of his index finger and whispered "Hey... hey... heeeey... It's going to be ok. Everything is going to be alright. Carl has given Uncle Tony one of his kidneys and you see he's fine right?" Juanita grasped Brandon's tear covered hand and said "I know but that's not why I'm crying. You see it all makes sense now. David has been plotting on taking this house for some time now. For months he's been boasting about how he was going to make some changes in Silver Pointe once that old timer is out of the way. He just kept saying all of these mean things about taking Silver Pointe by storm and it all starts at the beachfront. I never knew what he meant because he never shared anything of importance with me. But from all that you have just told me about how the house hasn't been generating money it all makes sense now. Brandon, David is part of the reason this place hasn't been doing as well as it has in the past. Or at least I think so. Before you do or say anything to him or anyone, promise me that you will give me a couple of days to prove it. I don't want to alert him and make him change up anything before we can counter his moves. PROMISE ME BRANDON!!!" Juanita could tell that Brandon was hotter than fish grease and was determined not to leave without him promising. Finally he blurted out "Ok...I promise. But you have exactly two days and that's it. After that I don't give a damn if you have proof or not, I'm going to beat his ass like I did when we were kids." Juanita smiled at the memory of the whipping Brandon gave David years ago. She leaned over and kissed him on the cheek and said "I know baby... I know" then walked off to her car.

Chapter 12

If it's not one thing then it's another

Later that night while sitting at the dinner table Carl asked Brandon "So now that the doctor has seen you he says it looks like everything should be a go. He says dad is doing better also so there may not be as big of a rush as expected. Normally it takes a few tests to see if someone is a good candidate or not. I'm glad he was able to get the test results of your blood type back in a day. That normally takes a few days also. Have you spoken to your job to see how it was going to affect you? I mean I don't want you to have to look for another gig behind all of this and all." Brandon smiled at Carl and said "It's all good cuzz. I've already spoken to my boss and let them know I was going to be taking an unexpected leave of absence. They are not tripping. As a matter of fact they give me and Uncle Tony their blessings. Syd was my only concern but now that she has let me know that she's cool, everything is cool." Just then William and Leslie walked into the kitchen with both of their hands filled with shopping bags. From the smiles on their faces everyone could see that they were in a good mood. "Well... well... well... if it isn't Silver Pointe's newest couple of the year. Looks like you two have been out and bought everything in town that you could. I take it you have enjoyed our small town mall? We were just finishing up our dinner but there's more than enough for the two of you. Have a seat and I'll fix you two a plate." Carl suggested with his eyes lit and a grin. "Wow we just ate at a little restaurant across town called 'Captain Cook's' right before coming back. I sure wish we had known. It looks like someone here threw down." William advised while rubbing his satisfied stomach. William reached in his back pocket and pulled out his wallet. He removed his credit card and said "I want to go ahead and pay for the remainder of the week. We've had so much fun here that we've decided to cancel our other plans and finish up our vacation time here." Carl stood and wiped his mouth with his napkin then shook William's hand and said "Boy you're alright with me. There may be hope for this old place after all. We don't have a way to charge a credit card but I feel I can trust you to go to an ATM sometime tomorrow." Leslie looked a bit puzzled then said under her breath "No way to pay with credit cards?" Then it appeared as though a light bulb came on in her mind. She snapped her finger and said "You know, I knew we came here for a reason. Every since we got here I have been racking my brain trying to figure out why no one else was staying here. I mean this is the PERFECT getaway spot. But since you said that you don't have a way to take credit card payments it's hit me. I hope you don't mind me saying this but… you all are behind on the times. I bet you don't have a website either do you?" Carl looked at Brandon and said "I have been telling daddy the same damn thing. We need a computer man. How else would we keep up with what's going on outside of these walls? No, we don't have a site because my daddy is afraid of anything that involves change. He is from the old school." Brandon scratched his head and asked "Are you kidding me? Are you trying to tell me that you all don't have a computer, let alone a site? Well damn cousin, no wonder business has been so slow. Hell no one knows about you man. Not to mention David's conniving ass." Carl's facial expression quickly changed with the sound of David's name. "Whoa! What are you talking about? What does David have to do with anything?" Carl questioned with a scowl. Brandon placed his hand on Carl's shoulder and told him "I had a talk with Juanita earlier today and she says David may have had some shit going on that's been harmful for business. She made me promise to give her a couple of days at least to get evidence. So just be patient and let's see what she comes up with and then we can confront him." William intervened and added "Well I don't know who David is but I know some people that know some people and we can get a website set up for you in no time. I also am in marketing and can get you set up with some of the major travel sites out there that would pay you for being on their sites." William then made a gesture as though he was looking around to see if anyone was looking or listening and jokingly added "But as far as this David fellow goes... I know some more folks that know some folks... that can handle his ass too." The three guys laughed it off until Leslie sucker punched William in the shoulder to show her disapproval of his comment in front of Sydney. "I appreciate the offer but trust me; we know how to handle David." Brandon suggested with a smirk. William winked at Brandon and said "Gotcha. Well we're going to head on up to our room now. We will see you good folks in the morning. Goodnight." The happy couple left the kitchen and headed to their room while the others watched them walk off.

After Carl and Sydney had gone upstairs to turn in for the night Brandon found himself taking a walk down the beach alone. He wanted to reflect on everything that had taken place since arriving back in Silver Pointe. He couldn't help for thinking about how good it felt spending time with Juanita and how Sydney seemed to get along with her. He kept looking up at the full moon wondering if she was at home looking at it also. He wanted to know if she was thinking about him as much as he was thinking of her. While thinking so hard about her his mind drifted back to when he was a senior in high school on his way off to college. He was back in New York sitting on his bed staring at a picture of him and Juanita in a frame from her prom. He was almost in tears when his bedroom door slowly eased open as his father slowly entered. He took a seat on the bed next to Brandon and held his hand out for Brandon to pass him the framed picture. He took a look at it and smiled then said "She a very pretty young lady son. I know that you two wanted to go off to college together and keep all of the plans you had as kids, but it's not the end of the world. Trust me when I tell you that this is not the end of the two of you either. One day in the future the two of you will have a chance to reunite but right now both of you need to focus on what you want to do until then. I know it's hard not knowing what the future holds but whatever it is, God's plan is greater than yours. He will see to it that the two of you see one another again somehow... some way." He handed the picture back to Brandon and placed his arm around Brandon then said "It's like the old saying goes 'If you love someone... Set them free... If they were yours then they will return... If not then they never were in the first place...' You have your whole life ahead of you man.

Live it to the fullest and trust that one day… she'll return." His dad kissed him on the top of the head then stood and headed out of the room. Before he left the room he turned to Brandon and said "As a matter of fact, why don't you give her a call and let her know how much you miss her and plan to see her in the future. I'm sure she's probably at home thinking about you the same way you're thinking about her. And don't worry about the phone bill. Tonight's call is on me." Brandon stopped him as he was leaving and said "Thanks dad. You always know just what to say." His father smiled and told him "Don't mention it. It's a part of your graduation present." His dad chuckled as he closed the door and walked out of the room. Brandon spent the rest of the evening looking at the picture while talking to Juanita on the phone.

While still walking along the shore Brandon's mind was all over the place. After reliving the lesson his dad gave him about letting Juanita go he then found himself back in college. It was his sophomore year and he was in the library studying for his mid-terms late one night when he looked up and saw her walk in with her roommate. It was Angela. He had seen her many times earlier that year but never had an opportunity or the nerve to speak. From the time she walked through the doors until the time she took a seat at the table across the room it seemed as though life was in slow motion for Brandon. He marveled at her beauty and was distracted by her occasional glances back at him. It was all he could do to try and concentrate on his studies. The more they looked at one another the more diverted he became by her. Soon time had passed by and the librarian was making the announcement that the library was closing in thirty minutes and to return or check out all books. With time running out Brandon didn't know if he was going to shit or go blind but he knew this was his best opportunity to approach her. He closed his books and gathered his things then walked over to her table. Nervously he looked into her eyes then extended his hand for her and said "Hi, my name is Brandon and I was wondering if I could talk to you for a moment before the library closed." Angela smiled and shook his hand and responded "Sure, I'm Angela. What would you like to talk to me about?" Angela's roommate got her things together and excused herself but before leaving offered "Hi Brandon. I'm Angela's roommate, Tanisha. I'm going to let you two talk while I check out these books before they close." Tanisha giggled and extended her hand for Brandon to shake also. He spoke and shook her hand but never took his eyes off of Angela. Brandon took a seat next to Angela. The two of them talked until the librarian came across the intercom and announced "The library is now closed.

Goodnight, everyone." Tanisha walked back over to the table with four other girls and placed her hands on her hips then said with a smile "Well I take it Casanova is going to see to it that you make it back to the dorm safely." Angela looked at Brandon for his response. Brandon looked up at the group of ladies and instantly knew that one wrong move and he would be smothered with insults and flying purses and book bags. "She is in good hands. I will make sure she gets to her room safely. I promise!" Brandon advised with confidence. One of the shortest of the group of young ladies stepped up and suggested "She better get there safely. Don't MAKE us come looking for you...lover boy!" The small group all laughed at her jovial threat then turned and walked off together. Although they all had a good laugh, Brandon knew they were also serious. The two of them walked back across campus to Angela's dorm. Once they got there they sat outside on the steps talking for hours just getting to know one another. They talked about everything under the sun from discussing their favorites to even their future endeavors. After that night they were virtually inseparable.

On his walk back to the house the closer he got he was brought back to reality by blaring headlights from a car parked on the side of the house. The lights were blinding but not so much that he couldn't tell that they were the headlights of David's black BMW. Cautiously he approached with his hands barely shielding the high powered beams. "David is that you?" he questioned aloud as he stopped nearly twenty feet shy of the car. The car door opened and out stepped David as he stood behind the door. "What in the hell are you doing over here so late? Is there something you need?" Brandon forcefully inquired. After a short moment of silence David belted out "Stay the FUCK away from my wife! This is the last time I'm warning you or else." Furious and upset Brandon yelled back "Fuck you!" David stood there for another second and screamed "I'm warning you. Stay the hell away. We are not kids anymore city boy!" Fired up and ready to tear a hole in David, Brandon began to walk up to David's car. David was just about to walk from behind the car door to meet Brandon when out of nowhere Sydney ran outside. She ran from the back of the house up to Brandon and wrapped her arms around his waist. She had tears streaming down her face and was trembling like a leaf. When David saw her he stopped in his tracks. He at Brandon and through his teeth he spat out "You got saved this time city boy but this is far from over. Stay away from Juanita and go back to New York. You're not wanted here." David got back in his car and sped off kicking up dust behind him. Brandon was so upset that he was trembling just as hard as Sydney. "Daddy what's going on? Who was that man and what was he talking about? Who is his wife and why does he want to fight you?" Sydney frantically asked with tears pouring down her little face. Brandon wrapped his arms around her and said "He's nobody baby. It's all just a big misunderstanding. Don't you worry your pretty little head about it one bit. Everything is going to be ok Rose Bud'."

Chapter 13
A rock and a hard place

The next morning Brandon got up before everyone else and left without alerting anyone. He jumped in his car and sped off out of the driveway kicking up rocks and dirt into an enormous dust cloud. Still fueled with anger and revenge Brandon had his mind made up that he was going to find David West and issue him a beaten like when they were kids. Driving around what was a relatively small town he realized he had no idea where to begin. He found himself riding around in and out of neighborhoods on a wild goose chase. While in the middle of having his epiphany he recognized the area as one of his favorite parks in town. It was the Freeman C. Martin Park only walking distance from Juanita's old childhood home. He pulled into the parking lot of a convenient store across the street from the park and went into the store. It was a locally owned and well known establishment that had been around back when Brandon's father was a little boy. It was the average corner market found in every urban neighborhood across America. The original owner, Mr. Watson, was an old friend of Brandon's grandparents and one of the first black owned businesses in Silver Pointe. Before he passed away he left the store to his son, Paul Jr. Everyone in the neighborhood called him PJ from the time he was a kid hanging in the store learning every angle his dad was working. He learned everything from how to run the store, to running numbers as well as the liquor house Mr. Watson had across town. The only difference in his liquor house and the others is that ninety five percent of his customers were white businessmen and officials that he had in his pocket one way or another. PJ and Brandon's dad were best friends from the first day they met in kindergarten until Brandon's father passed. PJ took his death harder than anyone but always stayed in touch with Brandon afterwards. When Brandon walked through the door of the corner store he was shocked to find that PJ wasn't sitting on his stool behind the counter as usual. Instead of PJ it was PJ's son Trey. Brandon and Trey were not quite as close as their dads were but they were really cool with one another and considered themselves as good friends. Shocked to see Brandon, Trey jumped up and rushed from behind the counter to greet Brandon and to show him some love. "Look what the north wind blew in. If it ain't New York's own my man K-Money. I heard you were in town. I've been waiting to see how long it was going to take for you to make your way around to these parts." Trey teased while patting Brandon on the back and laughing in his family trademark deep voice. Trey was a rather tall fellow and with a large naturally muscular frame much like his father and grandfather. They favored each other so much they looked like repeats of one another. Brandon took a seat on the stool on the other side of the counter while Trey took the other empty stool next to Brandon. As soon as Brandon took his seat a young lady entered the store looking like a model from a rap video. She was wearing a large floppy straw hat and a bright multicolored bikini top and a pair of Daisy Dukes that allowed the matching bikini thong to creep over the top of her low riding shorts. She walked past Brandon and took a seat on Trey's knee. She reached into her oversized multicolored straw tote bag and started to pull something out but stopped. At first Trey looked confused until he realized that she didn't know Brandon and wasn't sure if she should. Trey chuckled and told her "Oh that's my man from back in the day. He's cool." She looked at Trey then back at Brandon and questioned under her breath

"Are you sure? He look like feds to me! All straight laced and shit." She looked over the top of her Coco Chanel sunglasses staring at Brandon and chewing her gum as though she was trying to get every drop of the flavor out. Again Trey chuckled just before standing and nearly forcing the diva to almost fall to the floor. "Handle your business and I'll handle mine. Now give me what you came here for and don't ever question me again. Do you understand?" Trey barked at the clearly shaken bikini beauty. She staggered to her feet with her ankles twisting in her high heels like a newly born horse taken its first stance. Embarrassed and ashamed she straightened out her sunglasses and hat while she regained her footing. She reached into her bag and handed Trey an envelope bulging open with money. He snatched it from her hand and crushed the envelope and the large wad of money in the palm of his hand. He shook it at her and gritted his teeth and said "How many times do I have to tell you to get an envelope big enough to at least close it? You need to take some of that ass and put in your brain and MAYBE...just maybe you can then have some SHIT on your mind instead of trying to be a smart ass. Get the hell out of here and tell Man-Man I said he needs to see me before I see him. I know you know where he is too while you in everybody's business. Your business is in the street. Let me find out you covering for him and I'm gonna come over and pop goes the weasel." Trey's actions let Brandon know that Trey was definitely following in his father and grandfather's footsteps but with a bit more forceful manner.

Once the scolded young lady had finally cleared the building walking out with the little bit of pride she retained after her verbal lashing, Trey excused himself and stepped to the back office of the store to put away his money. When he returned he had two opened Heinekens for them to share. He extended one to Brandon to take. Considering it was still early, Brandon hesitated then said "Ahhh! What the hell?" He grabbed the beer and took a swallow then said "I see ain't much changed with yo crazy ass huh?" Trey smiled then said "Man I hate that shit. If I tell a motherfucker it's raining ice cream then get a cone and go get a scoop. She knows better than to question me man. So tell me New York, what brings you back to the sticks?" Brandon and Trey were finishing up a six pack by the time Brandon had finished telling Trey about how he ended up back down south and all about David and all that had taken place since he arrived. Trey sat on his stool and folded his arms then said with conviction "I can't stand that motherfucker!" Somewhat shocked and confused Brandon questioned with a laugh "Say what? You can't stand who?" With his face still bald up like a fist Trey answered "That damn David! I can't stand that sneaky bastard and he knows it. He's been going around town trying to buy up all of the properties around town so he can resale it. His low life ass knows that I know and it's killing him because my old man and I refused to sell. His bitchmade ass crosses the street when he sees me coming." Brandon was smacking the counter and laughing at Trey so hard he was in tears. Trey giggled but was just as serious as a heart attack. Trey continued "I'm serious man. That bastard has even threatened some of the older people out of their homes. I mean its one thing to sell because you want to but to be bullied is another. My old man isn't able to deal with all that bullshit now so you know; I took it upon myself to handle his ass personally. When my pops found out what dude was doing he told me what the deal was about. There's supposed to be some major developers coming into town within the next year or so looking to buy up land and putting theme park in town. It's supposed to be larger than Busch Gardens in Virginia. That would put Silver Pointe back on the map and bring in a lot of revenue but this bastard thinks he's the only one that knows. When pops told me that David came by here one night that he knew I wasn't here to talk, that's when I knew I had to go see him. After our little conversation and him changing his boxer shorts, he laid off of my dad and many others around town for awhile. I actually already knew that he was talking to your uncle but I never figured he would fall for any of David's offers. I don't know why I didn't expect him to lie to your uncle about some phony business deal. You see what I'm talking about? That fucker is slick. He knew he couldn't muscle your uncle because Carl would've torn him a new ass and then have to deal with you and Rusty. He had to find a way to run up under Mr. Tony" Trey suggested in disgust.

By the time Brandon finished telling Trey about all what was going on he looked at his watch and realized a little over three hours had passed. He down the remainder of his Heineken and tossed it in the large trash can behind the counter. "You need another one for the ride? I see you about to roll out." Trey offered as he stood along with Brandon. Brandon grinned and replied "Nah, I'm good. I won't be drinking anymore for awhile since I will have to keep my kidneys as clean as possible for Uncle Tony. But I will take a couple of cranberry juices to start flushing myself." Trey nodded and held his hand out towards the cooler for Brandon to help himself. He handed him a plastic bag and told him "Grab about four of them joints for ya self and four drinks for your daughter and Carl each. You know how we get down. You all are family to us. My pops wouldn't have it any other way, cousin." Brandon loaded his bags as recommended and dapped Trey on his way to the door. Just as Brandon was about to hit the doorway Trey said "I may have some dirt on ya boy David in the next couple of days or so. I just need to gain confirmation first. Check back with me in a couple of days. If my sources are correct, I'm going to make your trip down south more than well worth it." Trey had a grin on his face like an evil scientist. "I like the sound of that." Brandon advised as he nodded in agreement and walking out backwards. Brandon jumped in his car and headed straight for the hospital. He could hardly wait to see Uncle Tony so he could tell him all that he found out about David's low down ass. He raced through town just barely making the lights before they turned red. He slung his car into the parking lot of the hospital like he was driving the Batmobile. Brandon rushed up to Uncle Tony's room in a slow trot. He was nearly out of breath but really excited until he hit the end of the hallway of Uncle Tony's room. Walking out of Uncle Tony's room and headed in the opposite direction was none other than David West himself. He never even saw Brandon behind him, clear on the other end of the long hallway. Brandon took off running down the hall at top speed but David had already hit the double doors leading to the exit. He never even heard Brandon yelling for him to stop and come back. His first instinct was to keep running after David but ultimately he needed to look in on Uncle Tony first.

He rushed into Uncle Tony's room to find him surprisingly sitting on the edge of his bed frowning. Winded, Brandon asked "Is everything ok Uncle Tony?" Uncle Tony turned to him and yelled "NO! Everything ain't alright Brandon! Why are you bothering that man's wife and at MY house? I can't be in here concerned about what's going on out there. I'll never get out of here that way. So PLEASE for God's sake leave Juanita ALONE DAMN IT! I can't afford miss out on what I have going with her husband. I'm too old for this shit! Now he says you have been to her office and she's been to my house at least four or five times. Is that the kind of freaky shit you exposing that child to up there in New York boy? If so then you might as well leave her down here!" Brandon was shocked and at a loss for words. Every time he would attempt to open his mouth to explain Uncle Tony would shake his hands and head frantically saying "I don't want to hear it Brandon!" Brandon hadn't seen Uncle Tony that upset since he broke out Uncle Tony's truck window throwing rocks. He was sitting on the edge of the bed rocking back and forth but refused to even turn to face Brandon. Feeling hurt and betrayed Brandon bolted out of the room in raged. He rushed outside hoping that maybe he would find David lingering around so that he could release some of his frustration on David. When he finally got outside the only thing he found was the sound of the heavy rain beating down on the parking lot. Not finding David added insult to injury for Brandon. The entire situation had Brandon so lost and confused that he could only stand in the pouring rain in tears. Slowly he walked to his car with his head hanging low. He could only imagine what David could've told Uncle Tony. He finally reached his car but was soaking wet. He sat down and closed the door with force then began to pound on the steering wheel. The fact that he couldn't get a chance to defend himself was the hardest thing for him. He kept trying to think back to see if he could remember doing anything other than wanting her. Realizing they never even kissed or even mentioning anything of the sort aggravated him even more. The only real crime he was guilty of was reliving their good times.

Chapter 14
The pleasures and pains of love

Later that night Brandon sat downstairs watching television alone while Carl was gone out and Sydney was upstairs fast asleep. The sound of rain almost drowned out the sounds of footsteps on the wooden porch floor. Brandon slowly and cautiously approached the door and barked "Who is it?" even before the person could knock. The headlights and top fog lights from a Jeep Wrangler allowed him to see a silhouette of a raincoat with the hood over their head and a large umbrella. Brandon opened the door to find Juanita standing on the porch with tears running down her face from underneath her large sunglasses. She dropped her umbrella and jumped into Brandon's arms then began to passionately kiss him. Brandon held her tightly and caressed her back with his large hands. He forced himself to pull back from their love clutch and asked "What's wrong Rose Bud? Is everything ok?" Juanita held her head down and pulled back her hood. Brandon placed his finger under her chin and slowly raised it. Slowly and almost appearing shameful she removed her shades to display the black eye she was attempting to hide. A single tear dropped from Brandon's eye as he placed both of his hands on the side of her face for a better view. Once confirmed he put her face in his chest and asked through his gritting teeth "Did David do this to you?" Nodding her head she whispered "Yes!" Brandon started to walk her inside but Juanita pulled back. She said "I'd rather not go inside. I don't want anyone to see me this way. Besides, I don't want to leave my car parked in front of the house just in case David rides past. You know. But I don't want to leave either." Brandon thought to explain to her that the guest were out on the town and Carl was gone as well but he felt that it was just best to spare her the discomfort. Brandon looked off towards the stable and suggested "Ok. I tell you what. Pull your jeep behind the barn and let me just check on Sydney then lock up and I'll meet you in the stable in a minute. Is that ok?" She nodded in agreement then grabbed her umbrella and walked back to her jeep. Brandon waited to see that she got parked behind the stable and inside before running back inside to make sure Sydney was still asleep and lock up. The rain was still pouring down when he finally got everything he needed and trotted off to the stable without an umbrella to stay dry.

When he finally got inside of the stable he found Juanita in the loft laid back in a stack of piled up hay. He was impressed to see that she made it up there with no more than the light from the full moon hanging overhead like a balloon and shining through the large window used for tossing hay. Brandon made his way up to the loft to join her. His arms were filled with a bottle of wine, two glasses and a candle all wrapped in a blanket. "What's this? You brought treats I see. See I knew there was a reason I always held on to you." Juanita joked as she reached for the blanket so that she could spread it out for them to sit on. Brandon laughed and said "Noooow I get it. You only wanted me for the booze?" Juanita took her seat on the blanket then patted the blanket signaling for Brandon to join her. Brandon smirked at her but took his seat as instructed. "I brought a candle so we wouldn't have to turn on the bright lights but I see the moon is shining in perfectly." Brandon stated while looking deeply into Juanita's luring eyes. Her smile seemed to spell bound him even more. Juanita reached for the glasses and said "May I have a drink Mr. Smooth Talker?" Brandon smiled and pulled a cork screw from his pocket. He poured both of them a drink and buried the bottle in the hay to keep it from falling over. He took a sip and said "Now tell me what made that fool crazy enough to put his hands on you that way." Juanita took a sip from her glass and lowered her head. "He's pissed because he knows that I have been here to see you for one. He's also mad because he found out that I know about his business plans and the dirt that he's involved in." Brandon took another sip and said "Yeah that son of a bitch went crying to my uncle. I don't know what he told him but Uncle Tony is pissed with me. He wouldn't even talk to me today. I also went and talked to Trey earlier today. He told me all about David's little business plans. I already heard about how he's been forcing older people out of their homes." Juanita looked him in the eyes and said "Yeah but yesterday I found out that his sorry ass has been robbing your uncle and Carl. He's been manipulating the numbers when he is working at the bank. He has been increasing your uncle's interest rate on the 4th mortgage he has talked your uncle into taking out. He's been doing this to at least a couple of dozen people that have no idea what's going on because they have their accounts set on automatic withdrawal. The money is taken out of their account and the homeowners never question it. Meanwhile he is also hitting them with all kinds of bogus penalties and then when they get so deep in debt he comes to them with some trumped up business plan that he has no intention on following through. Earlier today he found the notes and files I have on him when he went snooping through my closet. He became so outraged that he slapped me twice. I took off running into the bedroom where I keep a .32 I got from my mother. He knew what was next so he left the house driving like a mad man. I left home because I didn't want to be there when he returned for one of us to end up dead somehow. So I came by here wondering if he was crazy enough to come over here. When I didn't see his car or yours I prayed that the two of you didn't see one another. I went to my office and parked out of sight just in case David came by looking for me. I took a nap in my office and when I woke up I had over 20 missed calls from him on my cell phone. He has left all kinds of nasty voicemails on my phone. I just stopped listening to them after awhile. That's when I decided to come over here to see you. I hate him! I hate him!! I HATE HIM! I HATE HIM! I HATE HIM!" Juanita cried out until she was literally crying again. Brandon held her and kissed her on the forehead to attempt to calm her down. Her tears were flowing like a river into Brandon's already rain soaked shirt. They kissed once again then closed their eyes.

Chapter 15

The art of war

In the morning the two of them were awakened by the sound of the stable doors squeaking when they saw none other than Rusty. It was Saturday morning and he was there to groom the horses and take them on a little ride along the shores to give them some exercise. It was something he had been doing for years and the only thing different now was his cousin was up in the loft with a woman. Brandon placed his finger over his lips to signal for Juanita not to make any sounds. Rusty had not noticed them and instead went about his normal routine. He walked deep into the back of the stable to retrieve some supplies. Meanwhile Brandon and Juanita rushed to get dressed before Rusty returned. Brandon was standing up putting on his shirt when Rusty reappeared from the shadows. He stopped in his tracks when he spotted Brandon. He placed the two buckets he was carrying on the ground and yelled up to the loft "Brandon is that you?" Brandon immediately stepped in front of Juanita trying to ensure that she remained hidden by him and the hay. "Yeah it's me." he yelled back at Rusty. Rusty scratched his head and started walking towards the ladder leading up to the loft. "What are you doing up there?" he asked Brandon. Brandon began to wave his arms frantically at Rusty saying "Wait! There's no need to come up. I'm on my way down. Just stay right there." Rusty stopped but had an extremely confused look on his face. "Why not?" he questioned Brandon. Putting his shoes under his arm Brandon rushed to the ladder just as Rusty was approaching the bottom of the ladder. By this point Rusty had figured out that Brandon wasn't alone and was beginning to have a little fun with Brandon. "You know I was actually coming up anyway to grab a bell of hay to toss down. It's no problem cousin." Rusty suggested while doing his best to fight back his laughter. Brandon began to stutter and got tongue tied but managed to spit out "Well just go back down there and I'll toss it down to you." Rusty couldn't hold it in any longer. He burst out into laughter and was doubled over at the look on Brandon's face. Rusty suggested "Look I may have forgotten some supplies back at the house. So I'm going to head BACK to the house to make sure I have everything." He put emphasis and volume on the end of his excuse for leaving the stable. On his way out he said to Brandon, "While I'm gone you might want to pick up behind yourself. The tenants and Sydney would like to go for a ride soon. So make it snappy and come get me when I can come back and prep the horses." When Rusty got to the stable door he stopped without turning around and yelled "Good morning Juanita!" Feeling a bit embarrassed and somewhat humored she yelled back "Good morning Rusty with your big head self."

Juanita finished getting dressed while Rusty was back at the house pretending to be looking for supplies. Brandon and Juanita walked out of the stable to find that the sun was still rising above the ocean. Brandon looked out across the ocean and spotted a familiar scene, it was the dolphins putting on the show that originally made the manor famous. They both stood spellbound while the dolphins performed their seemingly choreographed routine. As the dolphins swam away Brandon had an idea that struck him like a jackhammer. All of a sudden he was a ball of energy from nowhere. He placed his hands on Juanita's shoulders and asked "Do you need somewhere to stay? If so you are more than welcome to stay here." She smiled and advised "No I'm good. I have a small apartment across town that no one knows about except a couple of my girls but not even David knows. I'll be fine." Brandon looked out of the corner of his eyes and said "Are you sure?" She kissed him on the cheek and got in her Jeep and pulled off. He watched her pull off down the beach shore instead of getting on the main road. Allowing her to leave gave him a sense of helplessness. Once she was nearly out of sight Brandon took off running back to the main house. Before he could get halfway to the door he heard the next round of acrobatic dolphins putting on their aquatic show. Brandon turned his head to get a glimpse of the dolphins while still making his way to the house. Fueled with a newly found inspiration he sped up his trot so he could share his idea with his two cousins.

Brandon rushed up to the patio where Rusty and Carl were sitting at the table having coffee. Brandon was half out of breath and blurted out "Man I got it!" Carl yelled "Well I sure hope you didn't give it to her as long as it took for you to finally get IT!" Carl and Rusty burst into laughter. They were laughing so hard that even Brandon had to laugh. "See that's why I'm getting some new cousins." Brandon exclaimed while fighting back more laughter. Rusty cleared his throat in an attempt to act serious and said "Well what's got your panties all in a bunch cousin?" Brandon looked at Carl and then back at Rusty and noticed they were still fighting back the urge to laugh. "Don't even worry about it. You two are crazy." Brandon explained while still laughing himself. "No sit down man we'll listen. You know we had to give you the business. Now what's really on your mind?" Rusty suggested while nudging Carl with his elbow and trying to get him to stop giggling. Carl regained his composure and said "Ok... I'm sorry." Just as Brandon began to speak again Carl burst out into tear streaming laughter. That time all three were slapping the table laughing. Calming himself and fanning himself with his hands Carl smacked the table then asked "Ok cousin. I'm sorry. It won't happen anymore. I got it all out." Carl licked the tip of his finger and crossed his heart and said "Hope to die!" Brandon looked at Carl and still laughing asked him "What the hell was that for? Are we still nine?" They all chuckled again but finally got serious so they could talk like adults instead of grade schoolers. Rusty and Carl sat attentively while Brandon told them all about how Juanita found out about how David had been robbing Uncle Tony and Carl. He also told them about the conversation he had with Trey in regards to the new development coming to town. He also shared with them what he thought would be a hit not only for Dolphin Manor but for the city of Silver Pointe as well.

All he needed was to speak to William and Leslie to discuss a way to market his idea without it leaking to David. They didn't want him to get word of it too soon and try to sabotage their plans before they even got off of the ground good. "Well cuzzo, it sounds like you have just about everything worked out, but what about Uncle Tony? You know he is not going to like us doing all of this without speaking to him first." Rusty asked with a hint of pessimist in his voice. Carl stood and said "Don't worry about him. I will take care of that for us. It's time he and I have a little talk about Mr. David West and their plans. Once he hears about all that is going on behind his back, he isn't going to have time to worry about us. Besides, the biggest thing is to clear Brandon's name with dad. There's no telling what that underhanded ass David has told him." The three of them agreed not to speak of their plans to anyone outside of the family so they could ensure the secrecy of their plans from David.

Brandon and Sydney went to the local Wal-Mart and purchased a small computer system for the house. Brandon needed to act fast and needed internet access in order for his plans to unfold properly. Meanwhile he sent Rusty to run a few errands while Carl went to check on Uncle Tony and update him on everything. Brandon knew Uncle Tony was still a little upset and felt it would be best if Carl talked to him. Brandon spent most of the day setting up the computer and surfing the internet. William and Leslie walked in while Brandon had his face buried in the monitor sitting on the card table. William began to clap his hands and said "Congratulations for finally joining the rest of cyber America and not a moment too soon. Leslie and I took a few pictures around the house and different scenes around town. We were going to send them to our web guy and have him to add them to your new website. So whenever you get a chance I'd like to upload them from my camera and send them. I hope you don't mind us being a little forward by using ourselves as the so called models for your site." Brandon hopped up and grabbed William and hugged him as though he hadn't seen William in years. "Man you are alright by me. Hell no we don't mind. Now how much is all of this going to set us back? I know websites cost money." Brandon asked while still squeezing William. "If I tell you do you promise not to crush my shoulders anymore?" William inquired with a look of uncertainty in his eyes. Jokingly, Brandon looked at William and shook his head no, then said "But, tell me anyway." William thought for a second and wiggled loose from Brandon's grip it ensure he wouldn't have to suffer Brandon's excitement. "Well for the first year I'm going to cover the bill. It's the least I can do. After being a customer for a year you receive VIP pricing which is only fifteen dollars a month." William advised then quickly cringed to brace himself for one of Brandon's body crushing hugs. He slowly unballed himself when he realized that Brandon never moved. "You know I want to grab you but I'm going to refrain." Brandon explained with a huge smirk on his face. Brandon extended his hand toward the chair for William to have a seat. William cautiously took the seat while looking over his shoulder back at Brandon to be on guard for a sneak attack. Brandon chuckled and said "Man go ahead and take your seat. I'm going to fix myself a drink and step out back to give myself a break. When you get a chance you're more than welcomed for both of you to join me. Thanks man. I think this is going to be big for us. God sure has a mysterious way of bringing people together, doesn't He?" Brandon walked away from William and patted him on the shoulder and nearly scared William out of his seat. He exited the room laughing at William's antics and left the two of them to work with the pictures.

Brandon took a seat on the patio with his favorite drink while he watched the sun slowly set over the ocean. It reminded him of when he was a visiting for the second time as a kid. That was the year he discovered the true beauty of the ocean and to appreciate it. It was strange that he ironically discovered it, hundreds of miles away from the beach. Instead he found it in the hallway of the apartment building that he grew up in as a kid in the Bronx. Brandon took a sip of his cognac and closed his eyes. All of a sudden he was back in the hallway looking his old friend Sampson in the eyes. Sampson was a couple of years older than Brandon and some of the other boys he hung with when he was not in trouble. His mother was Black and his father was Puerto Rican. He was always in and out of reform schools for one petty crime after the next. He was always wearing an oversized green Army jacket and hoodie with black jeans and a Yankee's fitted cap. No one ever really knew where he stayed but he was always on the scene and always had money but no job. He was the typical poster child for the "product of his environment" campaign. He bullied most of the kids on the block except for Brandon. Even though he could easily beat Brandon as well as any other kid, he liked the fact that Brandon stood up for himself. So out of respect he never tried Brandon but instead would be willing to fight anyone for Brandon. The two of them would often talk in the hallway at night. He once told Brandon that he hated going home sometimes because of the fighting his parents did constantly. In a way he kind of envied Brandon for having a father that didn't beat his mother. He and Brandon sat on the back of a bench the first night Brandon came back home from his second trip as the sun was going down. "What was it like? Were there cows and shit everywhere? Did you see any of them fine country girls down there?" Sampson drilled Brandon. Sampson was the last person he expected to want to hear about a trip down South. He usually only wanted to talk about what was going on in the hood and what he would do if he was a professional athlete. Brandon laughed and said "Man it was nothing like that. I mean I thought the same thing before I actually got there. Now don't get me wrong, there are some places like that but my grandparents live on the coast. They have horses that they allow their guests to ride but it's not like they have a farm or anything. It's real quiet there too. I mean none of the loud noises like here and the smoky skies. It's a lot different than the city." Brandon could see how excited Sampson was getting from listening. He could tell that Sampson was imagining himself there. Sampson grinned and said "Man you're a lucky ass I tell ya. I've always wanted to go to a beach down south. You know? I want to go see the sky at night without all of the city lights and buildings. I read somewhere that they don't have huge skyscrapers and high rises like we do so you can see the stars and everything. I saw a brochure once that always kind of made me imagine how it would look. It had the picture of a white couple walking down the shore while the sun was setting. Then there was another picture of some fields and what-not. It just makes we wish I had some people to visit myself. Ya know?" Sampson stepped down from the bench and gave Brandon some dap and walked off. Brandon sat there on the bench and pondered on just how blessed he was to be able to see the sun rise and set over the ocean. It was then that he realized that he had just come from the place that some people could only dream about. He recollected the beautiful things and people he had seen down South that could not be seen in New York. He was brought back to reality by the sounds of footsteps on the patio and William's voice announcing "I'm done. Leslie is inside now on the phone with her people to get with some of the other sites once yours is up and running. My guy says he can have your site ready within the next couple of hours. Once you guys take a look at it and either approve or request whatever changes you may want, you will be ready to go live on the net." William took a seat next to Brandon and placed his drink on the table.

Chapter 16
Pillow talking

Late that night, while everyone was in the bed asleep, Brandon's cell phone rang and woke him. He reached over and grabbed it off of the night stand before it awakened anyone else. He answered without even looking at the screen to see who was calling. "Hello…" he said but no one responded. Half sleep and half annoyed he asked again with a bit of authority "Hello…" This time the voice on the other end responded with "Hey it's me, Juanita! I know it's late but I had to call. I hope you don't mind." Brandon sat up in the bed then cleared his throat and said "Of course I don't mind. Is everything alright?" She paused for a moment and there was silence on her end until he heard her say "I don't want to be alone tonight. Can you come see me?" Brandon grinned because he knew that she didn't just want company, she wanted to be pleased. "Where are you?" he asked as he was sitting up on the edge of the bed. Juanita took a big breath which was more like a sigh of relief. She said "I'm at my second place across town I told you about. This is my home phone I'm calling you from. I stay off of Hwy 258 South going towards Kinston. I'll text you my address. It's easy to find with GPS". He quickly freshened up and got dressed without awakening anyone. He rushed out of the house and headed straight for Juanita's. Brandon carefully followed her directions like a pirate with a treasure map until he was pulling into her apartment complex. Navigating his way through the huge complex he soon reached her doorstep and found the door unlocked as promised. When he walked through the door he heard the shower running. He didn't want to scare Juanita but he did want to alert her that he was inside. He said aloud "Knock... Knock... Helloooo..." Amazingly she was able to hear him over the shower and the music playing in the back room. Brandon heard the sound of her shower curtain rings sliding across its metal rod. Then from the bathroom he heard her reply "Come on in and make yourself at home. I will be out in a minute." Brandon removed his Yankee's fitted baseball cap and placed it on the coat tree behind the door. Her fifty inch flat screen television was tuned to the Lifetime channel. Brandon grabbed the remote and quickly changed to ESPN's "Sports Center" to catch up on the latest news in the world of sports. While removing his shoes, he realized the shower had stopped. He glanced over his shoulder when he heard her calling out for him to join her in the back room.

In the morning Brandon was awakened by the sounds of his cell phone ringing. He quickly grabbed it before it woke up Juanita. "Hello" he answered. "Boy you are slicker than cat shit on a linoleum floor ain't you? I'm not even going to ask where you are, because I already know. When you decide to tear yourself away Sydney and I are going up to see daddy at the hospital. You might want to join us. It's safe to come see him now. I've already calmed him down for you, but I won't tell him where you are and you might not want to either." Carl suggested on the other end of the phone. Brandon giggled at Carl's comical suggestions but took note as well. "I got you cousin. I'm going to make a stop after I run by the house to change and then I'll see you guys there in a few hours. Later." Brandon responded before hanging up. When he placed the phone back on the night stand Juanita rolled over and asked "Are you hungry? I'm about to fix some breakfast." Brandon grinned and answered "I'm hungry but not for anything that needs to be cooked." Juanita gave him an under eyed look and eased him back with her index finger in his chest.

After breakfast they got dressed and Brandon sat down with Juanita on the bed and said "I have been racking my brains trying to figure out how to help Uncle Tony save his business. After we spoke the other day and talking to the guest at the house, I think I may have it. It all started when I was looking at the dolphins and how your eyes lit up still. I think if we could remind people about the dolphins and kind of atmosphere we have we might be able to revive the place. I was thinking that we could throw like a huge block party/festival that starts just before sunset and last until sunrise. We could hire a band to play live music on the beach and rotate a DJ in every couple of hours. We could invite other venders to come set up tents and tables along the beach to sale their merchandise. We could let the kids ride the horses up and down the beach for a couple of dollars a ride. There's plenty of money that can be made to try and get Uncle Tony out of debt with David's punk ass. Then once that's under control I can concentrate on getting his ass out of that bank so it doesn't happen again." Juanita was grinning and clinging to his every word. She was just as excited about it as he was about telling it. "You know my class reunion is coming up on Labor Day. That's only a couple of months away. That will give you a bigger crowd in town. Not to mention a chance to remind people of what they left behind after high school. Brandon you may have stumbled across something here. As a matter of fact that has been one of the biggest buzzes on Facebook among my friends. Our committee has put together some lame day events but nothing really for the night life, not that there's much of one here. I'm sure plenty of people still remember you as much as you were down here. This is going to be great. I'm going online today and speak with the graduating committee and let them know we have something to do that Saturday night until Sunday morning! I bet if you talk to Carl and suggest he get in touch with the boys from his old high school fraternity they would really bring in a crowd. Back in the day they were the talk of the town. Carl and

Rusty both were in it." Brandon's eyes lit up with the thought of the possibilities. Fueled with excitement he rushed to his feet and said "You just reminded me. I need to talk to Rusty. He's checking on licenses and permits for liquor and parties. I'm glad you reminded me about their little group I remember them. It was about thirty or more of them. I can't remember what they called themselves though. All I remember is they had black t-shirts trimmed in grey with grey letters stitched on the chest." Juanita laughed and said "I'm sure you do remember them. Their name was Alpha Phi Lambda. You couldn't tell them anything either. But anyway, let me know what Carl says about them hosting a party and I'll get busy on helping promote the dolphin festival." Brandon kissed and thanked Juanita then left to begin the rest of his day.

Chapter 17
Thicker than water

After freshening up and getting back out Brandon made a stop back by the corner store to see his old friend Trey. When he walked in the bells tied to the back of the door rang out and Trey came from the back room zipping up his jeans. "Yo what's good my dude?" he shouted when he saw it was Brandon. He walked up with his hand extended to dap Brandon, but Brandon stopped short of Trey's hand. He told Trey "Man, no offense but you just came from the back room zipping your damn jeans. Not today dog. Not today." They both laughed and Brandon extended his forearm instead of his hand. Trey took a seat behind the counter on his regular perch and Brandon sat on the opposite side as before. Trey leaned over onto the counter and said "I take it you came to see if I had something for you on your buddy punk ass David West. Well I do and you are NOT going to believe this shit here. I have some photos of your boy that he does NOT want to get out. If you can't get him to fall back with these then I have a .38 that ain't never been shot before. You can toss it in the ocean when you're finished. But I believe these pictures will do the trick. Come back by here tonight around 9:30pm and I'll put a copy of them in your hands for you to see and have for yourself." Brandon nodded his head repeatedly and said "I can do that. Now how much does something like this cost me?" Trey stood and walked around the counter and said "Man listen, this is on the house. I would expose is ass myself but I don't have anything to gain from it. You on the other hand can make better use of them than I can. Besides, like I said before, you all are family. This shit right here is free." Brandon smiled and said "That's what's up. While I'm here too I want to let you be the first to know that my family and I are putting together a festival in a couple of months to try and bring in some tourists and business back to Silver Pointe." Trey slowly shook his head and stated "Now see that's what I'm talking about. Someone finally decided to do something around here. Yo let me know if you need ANYTHING to get this thing off of the ground. If you need some dough just let me know. As a matter of fact let me be the first to donate five g's down as a donation. Fuck it I'll write it off at the end of the year. If you need more than that then let me know and it will be a loan with no interest. You can pick the five up when you get the pictures tonight." Brandon could hardly believe his ears. "Are you serious?" he asked in disbelief. Trey looked him in the eyes with a straight face and told him "I'm as serious as a heart attack." While they stood there looking eye to eye the backdoor opened again. The same female that was in the store the last time Brandon was there walked out saying "I have to go. My husband will be home soon." Trey stepped to her and pointed back to the door. Without saying a word she turned and walked back through the same door. Trey watched her stomp away, and then he turned and walked back to Brandon. "Now that's whose hands you need to avoid! But I'm going to get back here and talk to her for a minute but don't forget to come back tonight for the pictures and donation." Trey suggested as he walked Brandon out of the store and onto the sidewalk. Brandon nodded in agreement and left.

After leaving Trey's place Brandon headed straight to the hospital to meet up with everyone else. When he arrived he was surprised to see William and Leslie in Uncle Tony's room with Carl, Rusty and Sydney. "Well... well... look at what the cat dragged in." Uncle Tony shouted when he was the first to spot Brandon standing in the doorway. Brandon was pleased to see that Uncle Tony was back to his old self and not still upset with him. He walked through the door and spoke to everyone then made his way over to Uncle Tony to lean in and hug his neck. Brandon held onto Uncle Tony for a few extra second to take in the love he missed after his last visit. While they were still hugging Uncle Tony whispered in his ear "I'm sorry I ever doubted you son. Now either let me go or you're going to have to take me on a date." Brandon patted Uncle Tony on the back then stood back upright laughing at Uncle Tony. "So now that the gangs all here, I take it you all have informed Uncle Tony of all that we have planned?" Uncle Tony shifted in his bed and said "They have told me everything and I should've known that low down ass David Jr. was a snake in the grass. You have my permission to do whatever you see fit to get Dolphin Manor back on its feet." They all sat down and began to plan out how they were going to go about carrying out their plans for the festival now that Uncle Tony was on board with everything. They discussed everything from where they could get food to party supplies. Brandon advised them of Trey's generosity as well as suggested Carl and Rusty reach out to their Lambda brothers. By the time they finished brain storming they had everything planned from a day festival for the families and kids to an all night white party on the beach for the adults celebrating their class reunion. Before they realized it the nurse was knocking at the door with Uncle Tony's dinner. "Mr. Patrick I have your dinner and meds for you." she kindly stated as she walked in holding his tray in one hand and his meds in her other. They all agreed that they would leave to give Uncle Tony some rest and let him eat in peace. When everyone was on the way out Uncle Tony asked Brandon to let him talk to him alone for a minute. Brandon stood next to the bed while Uncle Tony sat up and said "Listen, I know I was a little hard on you the other day but this shit here really has me stressed. The last thing I wanted to hear was that David's funky ass was around town harassing my little brother's son. You feel me? I know you were somewhere with Juanita last night. I'm not crazy. I mean hell she's grown up to be a nice looking young lady. I always thought the two of you made a good looking couple.

But up until Carl came and told me the scoop on her and David, I was concerned about you being involved with a married woman. It also made me look at her a little differently. But now I know that I didn't give you a chance to explain all of that yourself before believing David's dog ass! Can you ever forgive me son?" Brandon leaned over to hug Uncle Tony when he was stopped by the large hand of Uncle Tony planted in the center of his chest. He looked off and told Brandon "I didn't ask for all of that! I'll take that as a yes. Now leave with the rest of them and save our business please and thank you." Brandon laughed and said "You got it Unc." Then he turned and headed out to be stopped again when he heard Uncle Tony saying "Hey Brandon." Brandon turned to see what he wanted. Uncle Tony said "You know I love you right?" Brandon smiled and nodded his head yes. Then he said "I love you too." Uncle Tony frowned up and barked "See no one asked you about all of that. You're about to be the softest New Yorker that I've ever seen. You sure you from New York, boy?" Brandon just shook his head and laughed as he walked out and caught a glimpse of Uncle Tony chuckling to himself.

Later that night Brandon was sitting downstairs on the couch watching television when Sydney came and sat next to him. He put his arm around her shoulder and pulled her closer to him. She curled up tightly next to him and asked "Dad, how much longer will we be here?" He thought for a second and responded "Well Rose Bud' that's a good question. Depending on when the doctors say I can travel, it looks like I will be here for a little while. You on the other hand will be going back just before school starts. I've been trying to contact your Uncle Ronnie to see if he could let you stay with him for a little while until I'm well enough to come back home." Sydney sat up frowning and questioned "Uncle Ronnie? He has cats and you know I can't stand cats, daddy. Why not Uncle Phil and Aunt Mary? They stay in the Bronx too." Brandon giggled and said "He's about the only one of your mother's brothers that I would feel comfortable enough to leave you with. Besides Uncle Phil is never home and your Aunt Mary is too busy worrying about where he is to take care of her own kids let alone mine too. Remember last Christmas when Phil Jr. damn near set the house on fire because Mary was on the phone and not paying his little bad ass any attention? I told Phil not to have all of those damn kids with her baby making ass. Now look at him, six kids and a wife that doesn't want to work. Your Uncle Ronnie may have those two cats but at least they aren't subject to set the house on fire. Besides, he's cleaner too." Sydney cocked her head to the side and said "Now you have a couple of good points. I think the cats may be safer. But do you know what I was thinking?" Brandon leaned even further back and with one eye brow raised he answered "No but I have a feeling that you're going to tell me." She gave him a light sucker punch to the rib and said "Daddyyyyy! I'm serious. I was thinking that it would be cool if I got to go to school here for a year or the first half of the year; you know at least until you're completely healed that is. That way I can also help Ms. Juanita and Carl nurse you and Uncle Tony back to health. You know you would miss me anyway." Shocked and amazed Brandon asked "You have to be kidding me right? I mean, what about your friends back home? You don't have to do that, you know? This is not like New York baby. Trust me; I will be fine until I can get back." Sydney sat straight up full of excitement and energy. "That's the whole point daddy. It's not New York. It's different down here. I love how quiet and peaceful it is here. I mean it's only until you finish healing which is going to take at least six months or more anyway. Uncle Tony has plenty of room here for us. So, why not? Right?" she argued. Brandon laughed and pulled her back under his wing and suggested "You should go to law school. I'm not making any promises but we will see. We can't just impose on Uncle Tony and Carl. Not to mention the matter of schools and records. We will see big girl. We will see."

Chapter 18

Don't cut off your nose to spite your face

The next day Brandon and Sydney were in the car on their way to see Uncle Tony's doctor for Brandon's test results and updates. Brandon glanced over at Sydney and asked "Last night when we were talking you mentioned Ms. Juanita helping nurse us back to health. What makes you think she would be doing any nursing?" Sydney giggled a bit then smirked and answered "Come on dad. I mean really? I've seen how you two look at one another. I may be young but even I can see that you like her. Look at you smiling. Every time her name is mentioned you get a look in your eyes. I can tell she makes you happy daddy. I may be young but not that young." Before Brandon could respond he was forced to slam on brakes to keep from nearly running head on into a swerving black streak. When he came to his screeching and rubber burning halt he realized the car that came inches from ramming them was none other than David West! They both jumped out in the middle of the street and rushed one another. All Brandon could think about was how David had not only beaten Juanita but now put his daughter's life at risk with this stunt. "You don't think I know what you're up to city boy? Juanita told me about the little festival you and your family are planning. I'm here to tell you that you can cancel all of that shit. This is MY town! I was trying to be nice and all but now you're trying to take food out of my mouth. We're not kids anymore city boy. I'm about to teach you a lesson about coming into my town and messing with my money and my woman." David shouted as he stood in the middle of the street with both fist tightly clinched. Brandon was shocked at the fact that Juanita betrayed him that way. She knew that he was deliberately trying to keep it away from David until all permits were filed and plans set in motion. Juanita's treachery compounded the hate that fueled him. With his eyes bloodshot red and nostrils flaring Brandon took off for David just as David was lunging for him as well. The sounds of a blaring siren and blue flashing lights stopped the two warriors before they could collide into one another. A police officer pulled up and got out of his car. He walked over to the two steaming hot men and asked "Is everyone okay here?" Immediately David went from raving mad to a fake smiling politician. "Everything is fine here officer. We are just two old friends that happened to see each other and couldn't resist stopping. It's been almost twenty years since I've seen my old buddy." David explained to the officer. He knew David was lying through his teeth, but had no reason to hold either of them. He suggested "You two need to exchange numbers or something and break all of this up. You are obstructing traffic like this." David grinned and told the officer loud enough so that Brandon could hear "Oh I have HIS number already. Mmmmm hmmm! I sure do!" Brandon never said a word. He stared at David walking away until David was back in his car. "What the hell are you waiting on?" the officer asked Brandon with a blank stare on his face. Brandon got in his car and pulled away as well to avoid any further problems. As he drove off he whipped around when he heard Sydney say "I don't like that man."

Immediately after his appointment Brandon dropped Sydney back off at the house with Carl and Rusty. He rushed over to Juanita's to let her know just how upset he was with her. He pulled into her apartment complex on two wheels. He was so upset he could hardly see straight. He jumped out and ran to her door beating like a mad man. "Open up! Open this door NOW!" he yelled. With no response after several more strong raps on the door he finally realized that she was not there. He trotted back out to the main parking area to see if he saw her Jeep Wrangler and it was nowhere in sight. Even madder at not being able to show out, Brandon jumped back in his car and sped off nearly missing a parked car. Upset with everything Brandon decided he would try to clear his head with some time spent on the beach. He went back to the house and trotted out to the stable to take a ride on Biscuit. When he walked in he was shocked to find Juanita talking to Foxhole Freddie. He was feeding the horses while she was pacing back and forth talking more so at Foxhole than with him. She was grinning from ear to ear when Brandon walked up and asked "What are you doing here?" The look of disgust on his face was sharp and bone chilling. Juanita was shocked with his tone and surprised at the way he barked at her. "What... what do you mean? I just came over with good news about the festival. But I don't think I like your tone of voice Mr. Patrick." Juanita answered with a look of disappointment. Brandon stepped closer to her with his face balled up and said "And I don't like being stabbed in the back. I guess all those years of living with David's snake ass finally rubbed off on you huh?" With lightning speed she slapped Brandon before he knew what happened. Brandon's head spun around from her force but he smiled and said "Is that what you are used to with David, fighting like some alley cat?" He shook his head and watched Juanita stomp away in anger. Before she could get out of the stable he yelled "He told me how you told him all about the festival. Juanita how could you do me that way?" His words stopped her in her tracks. Slowly she turned around displaying a look of disgust of her own. She stomped halfway back and screamed "And is that what all of this is about? You think you can just talk to me any kind of way because of some 'he say...she say' shit you heard from DAVID? Are you kidding me?" She rolled her eyes at him then walked off mumbling to herself. After Juanita left Brandon stayed in the stable fuming from the betrayal he felt. He walked over to Foxhole Freddie and asked "Is Biscuit ready for a couple of laps on the beach? I need to clear my head". He held his head low and shook it from side to side then murmured under his breath just loud enough to get Brandon's attention.   Brandon looked confused and asked "I didn't hear you. What did you say?" Freddie looked over his shoulder at Brandon and said "You're wrong on this one. Just like when we had Charlie in the bushes of Saygon. I told Sgt. Kelly that girl won't no spy. She was innocent." Out of all of the years he'd known Freddie he had never heard him say anything of relevance. Although he knew Freddie was not working with a full deck he couldn't ignore the fact that his moronic rant raised some question of self doubt.

Brandon took Biscuit out on the beach for a stroll. While he was riding he couldn't help for thinking about the first time he went riding solo. He had ridden the horses before but someone was always with him when he did ride. Except for one early morning while everyone was still asleep, Brandon decided to take Butternut out on his own.

Butternut was his grandfather's favorite horse and wouldn't allow anyone else to ride him. He once watched his grandfather and Butternut race another man and his horse. Butternut won by over two horse lengths. Brandon had fed Butternut many times and granddaddy had even allowed him to sit on him a couple of times. Even though Butternut was the largest and strongest of all the other horses, Brandon didn't see what the big deal was about Butternut. He had been on nearly all of the other seven horses except for Butternut. So while Grandma Rose was getting dressed to head downstairs to cook breakfast, Brandon sneaked out without her hearing or seeing him. He raced down to the stable and saddled up Butternut. He carefully walked Butternut out to the shore and mounted him. About thirty yards into his ride a huge piece of paper flew past Butternut's face startling him. In a flash Butternut raised up on his hind legs and began bucking wildly. Butternut's loud neighing alerted Brandon's grandfather who just so happened to be coming out to feed the horses. Brandon held onto Butternut for dear life until finally he was thrown several feet off of Butternut's back. Butternut continued jumping and bucking with his feet barely missing Brandon by inches. Brandon feared for his life until granddaddy appeared from nowhere and grabbed Butternut's reins. He calmed Butternut down and walked him safely away from

Brandon. When he returned to Brandon he saw that Brandon's leg was swollen and not looking good. He picked Brandon up and threw him over his shoulder and walked with him while walking Butternut back to the stable as well. Brandon could tell granddaddy was not happy at all from how silent he was being. That's when he knew he had really messed up!

When he returned from the hospital he had a cast covering his entire right leg from his hip to his foot. When he and his grandfather walked through the door Carl, Rusty, Uncle Tony and Grandma Rose were the first things he saw waiting for him. When he looked again he saw that Juanita was standing in the back fighting back tears and smiling. They all rushed him asking questions about how he was feeling and what, when and why. Finally he held both hands up and rested his weight on his crutches to quiet the crowd. He said "One at a time please. First, I broke my leg in two different places. Second, I don't know what made me decide to ride Butternut. I guess I didn't realize just how dangerous a horse really is. But now I know." He turned to his grandfather with his head hung low and said "I'm sorry for taking Butternut out by myself. I know it was foolish of me and it won't ever happen again. Please don't hate me." Granddaddy put his hands on both of his shoulders and told him "Son I will NEVER hate you. I know that you think that I'm upset with you because I haven't been speaking to you but that's not the case son. I've been thanking God for you not being killed by Butternut. I don't know what I would've done if... I can't even bear the thought. I've never been so scared in my life than when I saw you lying on that ground not moving at first. Well anyway... I know that you have learned your lesson. I'm going to tell you like my father used to tell me... 'Pick battles big enough to matter, small enough to win.' Those are words you can live by." Brandon never forgot those words and did live by them. From a distance Brandon heard Sydney calling out to him. Quickly he snapped back and heard Sydney saying "Daddy... Daddy... Uncle Tony wants us to come to the hospital when we get out and about." Brandon whipped around and saw Sydney standing a few feet away.

Chapter 19
Pop goes the weasel

Brandon and Sydney arrived at Uncle Tony's hospital room and found him talking to his nurse. When he walked in Uncle Tony was grinning from ear to ear and the nurse was standing next to his bed holding Uncle Tony's hand. Uncle Tony's eyes lit up like a light bulb when he realized Brandon and Sydney were standing in the doorway. "Are we interrupting anything?" Brandon asked with a chuckle. Uncle Tony laughed and answered "I wish but no. Come on in. I was just talking about you and Juanita. This pretty little thing was just telling me about how she has to move from her new apartment complex because she keeps getting unwanted visits from one of the apartment owner's employees. She's even come home and found him inside of her apartment without permission. The second time she caught him in her underwear drawer. And you'll never guess who owns the apartment complex." Brandon looked confused but asked anyway "Who?" Uncle Tony grinned and blurted out "The BANK! And guess who the pervert little employee is." Brandon thought for a moment and it hit him. Smiling from ear to ear he kept repeating "I don't believe it! David West is a nasty bastard!" Uncle Tony was about to burst open with excitement. Brandon walked closer to the bed and Uncle Tony grabbed his hand and added "That's not all." He looked over at the young nurse and asked "Babygirl, do you mind telling him where you stay?" The young nurse was tickled at Uncle Tony's behavior and said "Sure. I stay in Shallow Creek Apartments like heading to Kinston." Brandon knew he recognized the name of the apartments but when she referenced the town of Kinston that was when he knew. He cocked his head to the side and said "That's where Juanita stays." Uncle Tony exclaimed "Exactly! Chances are he may already know that Juanita has a place out there." Brandon began to grow even more suspicious about Juanita and David. He wondered if maybe she was trying to help David bring down Uncle Tony and the rest of the town. It had been many years since he had seen her and began to wonder if she was the same Juanita he left behind years ago or was she a new Juanita that was bitter still because he did leave her behind. Although he could still hear Uncle Tony and the nurse still cheerfully discussing how they were going to bring David down, Brandon had tuned them out for the most part. He was pondering in his mind why Juanita would betray him and his family that way.

On the way back to the house Brandon couldn't stop wondering what were David and Juanita going to do to try and stop the festival. When he and Sydney pulled into the driveway Rusty's pickup truck was parked outside. He put the car in park and told Sydney "Go on in baby. I have something I need to do. Tell Rusty and Carl I'll be back soon." She nodded her head and got out. Brandon pulled off as soon as Sydney was in the house with a trail of dust behind him. In minutes he was across town back at Trey's store. He rushed in and saw Trey sitting behind the counter with his feet propped up watching television. Trey could tell Brandon was upset. "What's up cuz? You ok?" Trey asked with a serious look of concern. Brandon shook his head and responded "I don't know. My mind is all shot to hell right now. I just found out the one woman I've always thought had my back only stood behind me so she could put a knife in it. Man Juanita has been playing me. She told David all about my plans for the festival and everything. So I need to act fast. And considering I really haven't had much time to raise any extra bread... I was wondering..." Trey stopped him before he could even finish. He placed his hand on Brandon's shoulder and said "Say no more fam. I got you! Wait right here." He walked off to the back and left Brandon standing at the counter. After Brandon sat patiently for several minutes, Trey returned from the back with a small brown paper bag tucked under his arm. When he reached Brandon he stood in front of him and held the bag in both hands. He gave Brandon a blank stare for a few seconds then said "When I first told you if you needed more than the five stacks that I would LOAN anything else WITHOUT interest but considering recent events and having to get it on a rush... this is not a loan either." Brandon's heart was about to jump out of his chest. He thought Trey was going to ask for interest or something crazy. His relief was obvious. Trey chuckled and told him

181

"Listen, do not worry about paying this back either. Business has been good lately so I can stand to do this THIS time. I talked to my father about what you all are doing, and he already okayed it. He put in and matched what I donated. I think that with what you find inside of that bag, you should have enough to take care of everything." He slowly handed the bag over to Brandon. Brandon started to look inside when Trey stopped him and said "I'd appreciate it if you'd wait until you got home to open that up." Brandon smiled and nodded his head. He patted Brandon on the back and said "Now if you will excuse me. I don't mean to be rude but my show is on TV. Call me if you need me." Brandon laughed and walked on out saying "Thanks fam. I'll keep you posted on the progress."

When Brandon got back to the house he reached under his seat and pulled out the paper bag of money. When he opened it his face lit up from the shock of just how many bills were in the bag. He reached in and pulled out stack after stack of hundreds bound by rubber bands. He quickly rushed into the house calling for Rusty and Carl to come downstairs. When he didn't hear anyone coming down other than Sydney talking on her cell phone he asked "Where are Rusty and Carl?" She pointed out towards the back without even cutting off her phone conversation. He ran out back where they were sitting with their feet up and having a drink. He stood over the table and emptied the entire bag. When Carl and Rusty realized there were hundred dollar bills piled onto the table they both quickly sat up. Their eyes were as big as dinner plates. "What the hell? Boy daddy is going to kill you if he finds out that you are dealing drugs around here." Carl advised with a look of concern. Brandon popped Carl upside the back of his head and said through his teeth "I'm not selling drugs you idiot. I got it from Trey at the corner store." In unison, Rusty and Carl both responded with "Ooooooh!" Brandon continued saying "He gave me five thousand more the other night along with some pictures of David's punk ass. I'll show them to you later. You are not going to believe your eyes when you see them. This should be enough money for us to fund everything. All we need to do is get William and Leslie to go ahead and start promoting it online. The two of you can go ahead and start informing your classmates and high school frat brothers. The only thing we have not yet secured is a location to hold the white party." Rusty shouted "That should be easy. Mr. Conners has a bar and grill about half of a mile down the road that is empty. He was going to rent it out to a lady but her loan fell through before she could get going. The place is already set and ready for business. He was just telling me about it the other day. He says the only reason he even has the building is because someone was selling it for dirt cheap and he figured why not. He poured plenty of money into it getting it ready for her. Now he's stuck with a five hundred person capacity bar and no one to rent it. I'm sure he'd like to at least earn a few dollars rather than to just let it sit there doing nothing. I'll go by his place tomorrow first thing in the morning." Brandon nodded his head in agreement. Brandon clapped his hands together and started putting the money back in the bag. "Now that we know time is running out we need to get started before David and Juanita try to pull something." Before Brandon could say anything else Carl jumped in saying "Speaking of Juanita, she's called the house phone a few times looking for you. I told her to try your cell phone. She said she did but you didn't answer. Maybe she's innocent in all of this. Have you thought about that? I mean really? Otherwise, why would she try so hard to reach you if she already knows that you are on to her?" Rusty stood and headed back inside with his empty glass. Before he walked through the door he said "Yeah cuz. She's always been on your side every since we were kids. I don't know about this. I'm just saying…" Brandon looked at the two of them and said "Trust me. I know it's hard to believe but David told me stuff that only she knew. I don't want to believe it either, but tell me. How else did he know? The only other people that knew were the two of you. I know DAMN well you two didn't tell him. So who did? Exactly! That's why we have to act fast." They then heard the voice of William asking "Is anyone home?" Before long they were joined by William and Leslie. They spent the rest of the night brainstorming and making plans to start promoting as soon as possible.

With David being aware of what they were planning the three cousins along with William and Leslie's help, all took the next few days to begin promoting the festival. Carl and Rusty contacted as many of their high school frat brothers and began organizing the after party. William and Leslie returned to their hometown but continued to work with presenting the bed and breakfast to the top travel agents and websites. Brandon continued to ignore the calls from Juanita which he received daily. He refused to take her calls or even read the text messages she sent. His heart was crushed by her but he couldn't allow it to get him off track. He knew that the survival of their family business was at stake and he had to stay focused. Things were moving along fine and beginning to fall into place just like they needed. The website was generating plenty of attention and within the few days of running they had already began to get reservations for the reunion weekend. Once the word got out about the white party Carl and

Rusty's cell phones were ringing nonstop from their old classmates asking about the details. Before long they had created a buzz on Facebook and around town as well. The response they received was overwhelming to even Carl and Rusty. They were not expecting so many of the local business owners to be willing to jump on board with supporting the festival. They had nearly everyone in town preparing for the largest event the town had ever held. People were constantly stopping by the house and calling to confirm the dates a validity of the event. Everyone was excited at the new attention the town was getting even from neighboring towns. There were flyers even in the towns that were two and three towns away. The only person that wasn't excited was David. Rusty spotted him sitting in the barber shop as he passed by one day. David was sitting in the chair glancing at a flyer and then balling it up and tossing it in the trash.

Chapter 20
When two and two start to add up

With only a few days before Brandon and Uncle Tony's procedure everything was looking great and moving along as planned. The doctors had given the approval on all of the tests to proceed with the transplant. Based on their recovery time they would both be well enough to attend the festival but limited to doing no more than watching. Although they would be healed enough to be out and about they still would be too weak to lift anything or do any manual labor for months without risking injuries. That meant the two of them would only be able to sit and watch most of the festival's festivities. It was midday when Brandon and Carl were sitting in the kitchen discussing the plans for the festival when they heard a knock at the door. They heard Sydney open the door and saying "Hi Ms. Juanita come in. My dad and Carl are in the kitchen. Wait right here and I'll get him for you." Before Sydney could get to the kitchen she was met by Brandon with a blank stare fixated on Juanita. "What are you doing here?" he strongly questioned. Brandon took a look at Sydney's facial expression and realized his tone stunned her. "Sydney go into the kitchen with Carl and let Ms. Juanita and I have a minute." he ordered with a bit of embarrassment at his own words. Without hesitation Sydney exited looking confused with what was taking place. Once she was clear of the room Juanita walked towards Brandon saying "Listen, I know that you are upset with me but it's not what you think. I've been trying to call you to explain but you refuse to speak to me. This was the only way I could get to talk to you and tell my side of the story. I have something I need for you to see and hear." She reached into her large purse and pulled out a manila envelope and handed it to Brandon. "Take a look at these. Once you take a look at them and hear me out, if you still don't believe me then I have nothing else. But I think you will find that I did not and have not betrayed you in anyway." Brandon reluctantly took the envelope and opened it. Inside he found photographs and folded up legal papers. "What is this?" he asked. Juanita slowly approached him with her hands clinched together and answered "This is my proof that I didn't say anything to David about your plans. The pictures you see are pictures of David entering and leaving my apartment when I wasn't there. There're also pictures of him spying on the two of us together on the beach and everything. He has been bugging my apartment for months. He's set little recorders and hidden video cameras throughout my place. That's how he knew about the plans for the festival. Come to find out his bank owns my apartment complex. So he's been black mailing the manager of the complex to give him keys to the apartments out there and going into my place trying to catch me. After you accused me of helping him I hired a private investigator to do a little spying on him. It didn't take him long to find out what David was up to. On his very first day of the job is when he followed David to my apartment while I was at work. That's when he discovered the little gadgets that David placed in my place. Those papers that you have in your hands are his discovery of evidence documents and also my restraining orders against David. I'm just coming from the court house filing them not even an hour ago. I came here with this to prove to you that I would never deceive you that way." Juanita was a little taken aback when she saw Brandon lightly chuckling. "What's so funny?" she asked. Brandon smacked his empty hand with the envelope and its contents then shook his head and said "Wow! It all makes sense now. Just a few days ago another young lady working at the hospital just told my uncle about David's bank owning your apartments. She told us about how he was harassing her and others out there. I had no idea that YOU were one of the ones he was harassing also. I was convinced that the two of you were working together. I guess I should've known better. Can you ever forgive me?" Juanita's jaw dropped as she stood in shook at what she was hearing. "So you believe me then right? I mean you have to know that there's no way I could possibly be making all of this up right? I mean…" she asked with tears filling her eyes. Brandon nodded his head and she jumped straight in his arms and let her tears fly. "Yes I forgive you. Of course I do. I'm just so glad that you now know the truth!" she cried. The two of them locked lips as though it was their first time ever kissing.

Moments after the two of them detached themselves from one another Sydney and Carl came rushing into the room clapping and grinning. "Boy I'm glad all of THAT is over." Carl announced as he entered the room. Sydney ran in with tears in her eyes and hugged both Brandon and Juanita at the same time screaming "Me too!" The four of them all burst into laughter and taking a big sigh of relief. Juanita's cell phone went off in the midst of their celebration alerting her that she had a text message. She reached into her purse and began to read it. Quickly her joyful expression changed to a look of concern. Recognizing that Juanita was no longer smiling Brandon asked "What's wrong?" She looked at him and said "That was David. He just got served his restraining orders. He says those papers aren't going to stop him and that this wasn't over." She handed the phone over to Brandon so that he could take a look at the message. Immediately after reading it he dialed David's number and waited for him to pick up. It rang twice and David was on the other end cursing and yelling before Brandon could say a word. Brandon listened to his rant until David yelled out "Are you listening to me you BITCH?" Brandon walked off with the phone to keep Sydney from hearing him say through his teeth "You're the only BITCH on this call. When I see you that's exactly what I'm going to treat you like. And I'm not taking any papers out on your punk ass. So YOU are the one that needs to watch YOUR back! And don't think for one second that you are going to put your hands on her again! You sorry excuse for a man!" Before Brandon could say another word David hung up without saying anything else. Brandon looked at the phone and began to yell "HELLO... HELLO..." but there was no one there to respond. He started to call back and was stopped by Juanita grabbing his hand and saying "Just let him go. He's not worth it. Besides you need to concentrate on the festival. I'm going to head on now that you know the truth and all." Carl walked over to them then placed his hand on Juanita's shoulder saying "Oh hell no you're not either. You're staying right here until this is over. We're not letting you go back to that apartment for him to come over while you're there alone." Brandon looked at her and said "He's right. What if he comes over and you're not as lucky as the last time. You're staying here with us. I'll go back over there later and grab some of your things for you so you don't have to." Juanita's hands were trembling with fear as Brandon handed her phone back to her. "What if he does something to you Brandon? I'd never forgive myself." she inquired with tears streaming down her cheeks. Sydney walked up and wrapped her arms around Juanita and said "Don't worry about my dad. He can take care of himself. Besides, I could use another girl in the house with these two. I'm out numbered and they know NOTHING about hair." Her small intrusion was perfectly timed to cut the tension. Juanita wiped her eyes and held Sydney's face in both of her hands and said "Only because you asked. And I agree, these two no absolutely NOTHING about hair!" Juanita then looked at the three of them and nodded her head to show her acceptance of their offer.

The next night Brandon and Juanita were sitting out back talking when Juanita asked "Brandon do you mind if I ask you a question?" He took a sip of his drink and answered "Sure Rose Bud. What is it?" She shifted in her seat so she could look him directly in his eyes. "Are you scared? I mean scared of the operation that is?" she questioned with sincerity. He closed his eyes and nodded yes. She reached over and held his hand tightly. "Come take a ride with me?" she suggested. They jumped in her Wrangler and took off down the shoreline. "Where are we going?" Brandon asked after riding several minutes down the shore. "Just ride. You'll see in due time." Before long they came to a stop and Juanita got out and motioned for Brandon to join her. They walked about thirty yards away from the jeep and stopped at a large pile of huge boulder size rocks. The water was rushing up onto the rocks and crashing into them with tremendous force. She started to climb up the pile of rocks and again turned to motion for Brandon to follow her. "It's ok. Trust me. Follow me. I want to show you something." Cautiously Brandon followed behind her as they both balanced themselves on the rocks while the lights from her jeep lit their path. Once they reached the peak of the pile they stood together hand in hand on a huge flat boulder. "Do you recognize where we are?" she asked. Brandon looked around and said "Yeah. We're standing on a pile of rocks on the shore and getting WET!" Juanita giggled and said "No silly. I mean do you not remember this place?" Brandon surveyed the area again and just shrugged his shoulders then said "I give up. Where are we?" Juanita smiled and looked up over their heads and pointed. "This is where we first met. Except for we were way up there instead of down here. You see that day you saw me standing on the rocks above us, you thought I was going to jump to my death. You came over and told me not to jump. Do you remember that?" Brandon looked as though he was reliving the day all over again. "Awww, man. You're right. I just knew you were about to kill yourself. I felt like a fool when you told me you weren't even thinking about anything crazy like that." Brandon stated as he chuckled until he realized Juanita wasn't laughing with him. His expression quickly changed to confusion mixed with concern. "Wait a minute. Are you trying to tell me..." he said looking at her then back up to the cliff above. He lowered his head and she nodded her head and said "Yeah. I was saying my prayers and asking God to help me. I had looked down here and picked a spot to land. This is that spot. You see, God did help me. He sent me you Brandon. Had you been even a minute later you would have been too late. I had already made up in my mind that I was not going back to that house with my mother and father to put up with their fighting. You saved my life that day Brandon. I didn't want to ever tell you because I was too embarrassed at the fact that I even contemplated such a foolish act. Every since that night if I ever got scared, confused or just needed courage I'd come here and think of you and how you saved my life. I brought you here tonight so that you too could hopefully find courage as I do." Brandon's heart was pounding like a drum as he listened to her and remembered that day. Speechless and shocked he took a seat on the rock. A tear rolled down his cheek as he thought about the possibilities of what could have happened had he not gotten there in time or chose not to stop period. Juanita took a seat next to him. She put her arm around him then placed her head on his shoulder as they both sat there quietly taking in the moment.

Chapter 21
Hit the fan

The next day Brandon spent most of the day hanging with Uncle Tony at the hospital talking to doctors to prepare for their surgery. On his way back to the house he received a call from Juanita. "Hello!" he answered. "Hi baby. Do you still have my key to my apartment from the other night when you grabbed some of my things?" Juanita asked. He thought for a moment and answered "Yeah as a matter of fact I do. I have it on my key ring because I didn't want to lose it. I'll give it back to you when I get back." Juanita laughed and responded "That's fine sweetie but I was actually calling because I need my laptop from my bedroom. Do you mind stopping by there and grabbing it for me? I have some dental insurance claims I need to make sure were processed since I haven't been in the office lately." Brandon answered "Sure baby. I'll head there now and grab it for you. I'll see you guys when I get there. You, Sydney and I can ride out to grab a bite to eat when I get back. Bye beautiful." They hung up and Brandon headed to Juanita's. Not long after getting off of the phone with

Juanita, Brandon pulled into her complex to carry out her request. On his way out of the apartment with Juanita's laptop bag on his shoulder he was stopped dead in his tracks before he could reach his car. His eyes grew the size of watermelons when he realized he was standing less than ten yards from none other than David West himself. Since being back in Silver Pointe he had only seen David in his tailored suits with his briefcase. Instead of his normal attire he stood before a much more dress down David in a pair of gym shorts, t-shirt and tennis shoes. He looked as though he had been to the gym working out but Brandon knew better. Brandon took a quick glance around the parking lot in search of David's BMW which was nowhere to be found. This let him know that David had been somewhere lying in wait for someone to come back to Juanita's place for one reason or another. With no one around to get in the way to stop them Brandon carefully placed Juanita's laptop bag on the ground and began to walk towards David. With an equal amount of hate in his eyes David began to move towards Brandon as well. As they got closer the two combatants charged one another full steam. In a flash David dipped down and scooped Brandon off of the ground and tossed him over his shoulder and to the ground. Brandon's body hit the concrete with great force. Slowly he rolled over to get up but not before receiving a swift kick to the stomach from David. "Come on you motherfucker!" David yelled. He then kneed Brandon in the nose just as Brandon was getting off of the ground. The powerful blow stood Brandon straight up and resulted in a blood spattering reality check. Shaking his head to clear the cobwebs Brandon realized he was going to have to give it his all if he wanted to come out on top in this fight. "Is that all you got, you pussy? Bring it!" Brandon demanded. He staggered a couple of steps towards David then put his fists up to prepare for the real battle that was coming. Fueled with hate and anger David charged Brandon swinging both fists. Brandon dodged the first two punches then threw one of his own that landed in the right eye of David. Then he followed that punch up with a quick left jab to David's mouth with pin point accuracy. David rocked back on his heels and was spun around from the powerful combination. With cat like reflexes Brandon quickly jumped onto David's back and slipped his arm around David's neck and began to choke him. Desperately, David reached back and dug viciously into Brandon's eyes. Like a pit bull, Brandon refused to release his grip, even with David clawing wildly at Brandon's face. Shaking his head fiercely David was able to loosen Brandon's choke hold. That allowed David to shoot Brandon two quick blows to the gut with his elbow to free himself completely from Brandon's grip. Gasping for air David stumbled a few feet away from Brandon who was also gasping for air. Coughing and grabbing his neck, David shouted "Why couldn't you just leave us alone? I hate you." Doubled over and breathing heavily Brandon responded "Fuck you. I hate you too!" David rushed towards Brandon running full speed and was quickly met with a jaw crushing right punch that was followed by a left hook to his nose. Dazed and staggered David stumbled backwards then fell on his ass. Brandon got a running start and kicked him in the center of his chin with all of his might and said "That was for Juanita. And I don't want to hear from your ass anymore. You hear me? Also you're going to leave my uncle alone too." Brandon stood over David's defeated and beaten body while he writhed in pain and anguish from his whooping. Satisfied with his work Brandon began to walk away and left David lying on the ground nearly unconscious.

When Brandon pulled into the driveway he was met by Juanita and Sydney before he could turn his car off. On the way back he did his best to try and clean up but there was no hiding the bruises he sustained from his brawl with David. When he stepped out of the car they both noticed his scarred face. "Daddy what happened to you?" Sydney inquired with sincere concern. Juanita followed with "Oh my God. Look at your face. Who did this to you?" They both helped him into the house as he began to explain what happened. Carl was coming down the steps just as they were entering the door and saw them assisting Brandon. "What the…" he started to say when Brandon stopped him. "Let's just say I look and feel a hell of a lot better than David West's ass does. I will tell you all about it. I don't think we will be bothered by him for a looooong time, if he knows what's best for him." For the next hour or so Brandon told them all about his battle with David while Juanita nursed his wounds. When he finished getting worked on at the house they all agreed that he should contact Uncle Tony and his doctors to inform them of what had taken place. With his procedure coming up in two days they didn't know if he would still be fit for surgery. After speaking to the doctor's nurse he was asked to come in for a quick evaluation to make sure there were no damages to any of his organs that could affect his kidneys from functioning properly. Juanita drove him to the hospital so he could be checked out as directed while Carl and Sydney stayed behind. It didn't take long for them to determine that there was no internal bleeding or malfunctioning to prevent surgery as scheduled. Once Brandon was finished getting evaluated they headed straight for Uncle Tony's room to see him next.

When he walked through the door of Uncle Tony's room the first thing he said to Brandon was "Damn if you look that bad I'd hate to see David. What did the doctors say?" Brandon limped his battered body in and took a seat in a chair next to Uncle Tony and said "Well, I hurt like hell, but they said I'm ok to proceed with the surgery as planned. So in a couple of days we will be on surgery tables next to one another still." Uncle Tony grinned and looked at Juanita and asked "Baby do you mind giving us a moment alone to talk in private?" Slowly she stroked Brandon's head and answered "Sure Mr. Patrick." As she was turning to walk away Uncle Tony told her "Um Juanita, you can call me Uncle Tony like the rest of the family." She smiled and trotted back to his bedside with a hug and said "Yes Uncle Tony and thank you." She then walked out and closed the door behind herself. Brandon smiled and told him "That meant a lot to her and me both Unc. Thanks for accepting and approving of her." He looked at Brandon and said "She was and has been family long before today. And that's part of what I wanted to speak to you about. You know that she has been with David for some years now. I have seen them together around town for many years here and there. She is a good woman and deserves a good man like you, but I got a call from David's attorney not long before you got here. He is pressing charges against you for today's fight. He is claiming that you attacked him and is trying to break up his marriage. I just don't want there to be a problem with Juanita having to choose sides. I know she has loved you since you guys were kids, but people change over the years, son. The only reason David's lawyer contacted me before they served the warrant is because he and I are old high school friends. David doesn't even know he called me. Now there's nothing he can do about them serving the papers against you but he wanted me to at least let you know so that you can be prepared. This is just David's attempt to shut down the festival and all of the hard work that you all have put in towards getting everything together. He knows there is nothing that he can do now to stop it so he's reaching. To tell the truth he might have something here if he starts trying to use Juanita against you and she sides with him for whatever reason." Uncle Tony could see the look of concern on Brandon's face and added "Son it's not that I think she will mean any harm but I just don't want her to feel backed into a corner and obligated to side with David if they mention 'Common Law Marriage' to her. She has been with him long enough that they don't have to have a ceremony to be considered his wife in the state of North Carolina. All it takes is one full year of cohabitating and she is his. After that even if she wanted to help, she appears to be no more than a scorned wife looking to get even with an asshole of a husband. I'm sorry son but we may have a problem here." Brandon's spirits were visibly shattered at Uncle Tony's realization. Feeling dejected and frustrated Brandon left Uncle Tony's room to return back to the house with Juanita.

On the way back to the house Brandon began to think about everything that he and Uncle Tony discussed in the room. His awkward silence made it apparent that something was weighing heavily on his mind. Unsure if she should ask Juanita decided to question it. Unable as well as unwilling to hold it in any longer Brandon told her everything Uncle Tony told him. He even told her about his concerns about her not wanting to get David in trouble considering she never pressed charges in the past. By the time he finished they were pulling into the driveway to the house. Juanita put the car in park and turned to him to say "Listen, I can understand you not knowing what David is going to do but you have to trust that I am by YOUR side now and NOT his. I always have been and I always will be. It was no coincidence that we got back together Brandon. We are meant for one another. I know this is a bit fast but...I love you! I fell in love with you that day on the cliff when we first met. I love you so much that I've only been with two men in my entire life. Well one actually, I don't know if I can call David a man now." Brandon smiled and said "I know that all of that is true and everything but I can't help for wonder why in the hell did you even stay with him for so long if you don't have feelings for him somewhere?" She slowly and shamefully shook her head and answered "I was scared. Scared of him, scared of change, leaving and just down right out scared of life period Brandon! It wasn't until you returned that I remembered that I am worth so much more than he ever allowed me to be. The truth is, I should have BEEN out of this town but I stayed because I felt that I had to take care of my mother. I know I should have packed my things after she passed but like I said...I was scared Brandon. I didn't know what to do or where I would go." Brandon placed his hand on the side of her face and gently stroked it then asked "What about now Juanita? Are you still scared?" She placed her hand on his stroking hand then said "As long as I have you on my side I'll never be scared of anything or anyone again." The two of them passionately kissed until the front door of the house flew open and Sydney and Carl both came out running!

The two of them charged the car talking a mile a minute trying to tell him the same thing. "Whooooaa! What's going on? One at a time. I can't understand the two of you talking at the same time." Brandon suggested. Half out of breath Carl blurted out "That punk ass David has been here with the police talking about how you jumped on him and he was pressing charges and what not. He was saying how there wasn't going to be a festival with you locked up in jail because he was going to tell everyone in town about how it was being run by a thug out of New York. I wanted to kick his ass again, but you know…that policeman was there and he had a gun and everything so I told him to get the hell off of my property with all of those lies. Luckily the officer was cool about it. He says all you have to do is either turn yourself in or he could just come back here tomorrow. I told him only guilty people turn themselves in and my damn cousin ain't GUILTY! So tomorrow when they come back they will have a nice surprise waiting on them. I've already called Johnny Mack and told him I need him and all of his legal talking ass here first thing. He said he will be here around 8 o'clock in the morning. I told him make it seven damn it! And he will be here at seven…WAITING! I'm hotter than fish grease at this punk ass David. Now I'm sick of him. Johnny said it's David's word against yours and doesn't have a case. Uuuuuuu I can't wait to see the look on his face when he sees Johnny Mack. Everybody in town knows Johnny Mack don't PLAY! Just like everybody in town knows it's a FACT that Johnny Mack knows his shit and is a GOOD friend of the family. We going to settle this thing once and for ALL! I told him EVERYTHANG about David's girl boy ass from him trying to trick daddy and bully others to how he was stalking and EVERYTHANG! Johnny Mack is gon get his ass, you watch! He messed with the WRONG one NOW! I'm gon tell him, GET HIM JOHNNY MACK…GET HIM!" Carl was so animated and worked up with his facial expressions and hand gestures that he became more comical to the three of them than anything else. Brandon slowly got out of the car and put his hand on Carl's shoulders to stop him from bouncing around and shadow boxing then said "I'm going to need you to calm DOWN! You are acting like your daddy right now. So relax and breathe before you end up in the hospital with Uncle Tony in bunk beds together." Carl did all he could to hold back his laughter but couldn't. He and the rest fell out laughing at Brandon. "Shut up before I call Johnny Mack and tell him not to worry about it." Carl said laughing at himself.

Chapter 22
When all of the smoke clears

Early the next morning Carl was up with breakfast cooking and waiting for Brandon to wake up and join everyone else in the kitchen. When Brandon finally came down he realized there was not only Carl, Juanita and Sydney waiting but also Johnny Mack, Rusty and a guy he had never met. He walked through the kitchen door and saw Carl grinning like the cat that swallowed the canary. "C'mon in cuzz and get you something to eat. Let me introduce you to Silver Pointe's own Mr. JOHNNY MACK himself!" Brandon walked over to the gentleman wearing the Sears Sucker suit and white brim and shook his hand. He was a light brown skinned older fellow with a raspy voice and long wavy white hair that peeked out from his brim. "I've heard a lot about you young man. Your father and I were fishing buddies among other things before he passed away. I miss that card playing SOB. We had plenty of good times together when we were kids. Don't you worry none. That low down David West doesn't have a leg to stand on. And from what I hear you knocked him off both of them twice now. By the time I'm through with him he'll be lucky to have a tail left to sit on." Johnny told him. Brandon laughed as Rusty approached him with a guy that stood just as tall as Rusty did but even more muscular and a head full of dreadlocks. Brandon looked up at the guy and said "Let me guess, you're here to eat David if he gets out of hand?" Everyone including the guy fell out laughing at Brandon's remark. The guy extended his hand for Brandon to shake and said "No I'm Damon the bondsman. I'm here to make sure that if you do have to go downtown that you don't even see the holding cell let alone a jumpsuit." Rusty patted Damon on the back and added "Damon is my old personal trainer also. He helped me rehab when I had my injury and we have been friends ever since. I called him last night and told him what was going on and he came just for backup. But that was before I knew Johnny Mack was coming. But since he's here he might as well hang around." Brandon shook Damon's hand and said "Well thanks for coming brother but um…feel free to eat David's ass if you want."

Not long after the laughter stopped there was the much awaited knock at the door. Like a herd of wild animals everyone rushed to the door with their game faces. "Who is it?" Carl barked at the door. A voice on the other side responded "You know who the hell it is Carl now open up. I have the police with me and we want that damn cousin of yours." That's when they heard another voice on the other side saying "Mr. West I have asked you to let me do my job. I do not need your help. Now please step back or it will be YOU who goes into custody for obstruction of justice." That was when Carl opened the front door with everyone giggling at the way the officer had to scold David. The officer said to Carl "Good morning sir, I'm

Officer Stan Jones with the Silver Pointe Police Department. Are you Brandon Patrick?" Before Carl could respond Brandon stepped from the back of the crowd and said "No sir he's not. I am. What can I do for you?" Not much taller than five foot eight the officer found himself looking up at both Rusty and Damon in amazement of their height and build. Their sizes both confused and unnerved the officer to the point that he was nearly at a loss for words. While the officer was stuttering and trying to get his words together Brandon leaned over to Sydney and whispered something in her ear. In a flash she took off upstairs without question. Annoyed at the officer's unprofessionalism Johnny Mack stepped to the front. He said to the nervous officer "Listen let's just get down to business. I'm Mr. Patrick's legal aid in this matter and we are fully aware of why you are here. In fact we not only refute these outlandish accusations against my client but demand that Mr. West drop this charade at once or else." Attempting to prove that he was not moved by Johnny Mack's threat nor the Brandon's backup David blurted out "Or else WHAT? His ass is going to JAIL today and I'm not dropping shit. I know who you are and I know about your reputation. As far as I'm concern you don't have ANYTHING on me old man. So, now what?" Boldly and sure of herself Juanita stepped forward as Brandon tried to hold her back she snatched away from him and shouted "He may not but I damn sure do. For years I have allowed you to treat me like a dog. You have beaten me both physically and mentally without me saying a WORD to the police. But no more! You sorry limp dick COWARD! I have the bruises here in my face still to prove it and the pain in my heart to follow through. If anyone goes to jail here today it's YOU! You no good DOG. My restraining order says you are far too close to me even now! You should have left when you had the chance." Juanita reached into her purse and pulled out her papers and offered them to the officer and said "Officer arrest this man. Even with you here I am in fear of my safety." Desperately David responded "I knew your ass was over here. How in the hell can you have a restraining order against me when we are married and living under the same roof? Think you simple BITCH! You are in a common law marriage. That means you are MINE! "David laughed and stuck his chest out like a proud peacock.

While the officer perused the paperwork for legitimacy Johnny Mack added "Oh you're going to jail. It might not be today or even tomorrow but your ass is going. By the time I finish filing extortion, tampering with federal files at the bank, aka embezzlement, and communicating threats to the seniors of the town, and a list of break in and entering complaints from tenants from the apartment complex your former employers own along with any and EVERYTHING I can find to throw at you…oh yeah…your ass is going away from HERE! You disrespectful low life piece of…" Before Johnny could finish David lunged as though he was going to attack but was stopped by the officer while he was still reading the restraining order. He advised David "Hold on there Mr. West. The address on here says she lives at one address and you live at another. Common law marriage says you have to be residing in the same home for 365 consecutive days first of all. So if she has spent even ONE night away from your common dwelling then the common law marriage starts over each time she returns. However, unfortunately for you the state of North Carolina does not recognize common law marriages as legal and binding. Apparently she is right. You are in DIRECT violation of this order." The officer pointed at the papers with his finger and said "It says right here that you…David West…are too close. And because you said so yourself, and I quote 'I knew your ass was over here' unquote lets me know that you didn't just happen to come over here and find that she was here by mistake. You knowingly came here with prior knowledge that she would be here. Married or not you are under arrest. You need to turn around and put your hands behind your back. You have right to remain silent…and I suggest that you do. You have the right…" David yelled out "What about him? You need to be reading him his rights and locking him up also. He assaulted ME!" The officer took another look at Rusty and Damon then said "I only have one set of handcuffs. You have the right to an attorney…" he continued reading David his rights as he walked him off of the porch and to his police cruiser. David looked back and yelled "This ain't over Brandon Patrick. Do you hear me? This is NOT over!" The officer placed David in the car just as Sydney was returning from upstairs with Brandon's briefcase. "I finally found it daddy but I missed everything. Dang it!" Brandon took the briefcase and jogged out to the officer's car. David laughed and said "That's right you might as well get yo ass in here too." Brandon sat the briefcase on the hood of the car and asked the officer "Do you mind one moment before leaving?" The officer shook his head no and allowed Brandon to proceed to reach in and pull out the manila folder with the pictures he got from Trey. The officer followed Brandon to the back window of his cruiser to see what he was doing with the envelope. Brandon reached in and pulled out five enlarged photos and told David "Now unless you want these pictures to float around town, I suggest you not only drop this bullshit assault charge but leave my family AND Juanita the hell alone forever. You got that?" The officer stood closely behind Brandon looking over his shoulder at the photos and lost his breakfast at what he saw. Meanwhile everyone back on the porch except for Carl and Rusty were wondering what was Brandon showing David that would make the officer puke all over the place. Damon along with the others had a confused look on his face asked "I don't get it. What's going on?" Carl was doubled over in laughter and unable to speak. Rusty took one look at Sydney and spared the details and said to them "Let's just say he has proof old David can make a cucumber disappear like magic! And trust me, he's no magician either." With hearing that, Carl doubled over in laughter. Brandon walked back to the porch with his briefcase in hand and left David in the police car cursing and calling him every name but the child of God! When he got back to the porch everyone was in tears laughing except for Sydney. Her young mind was just not ready! They all walked back into the house with her shaking her head saying "I don't get it. Let me see!" In unison they all yelled "NO!" and burst into laughter even harder as the policeman pulled away with David in the backseat still cursing loud enough to be heard back in the house.

THE END

Epilogue

The morning after David was carted off to jail from Dolphin Manor Brandon and Uncle Tony went through the procedure without any complications. They were both well taken care of while in and out of the hospital. While they were both still at risk of injury they took full advantage of their chances to lie around and be waited on hand and foot. Early in the evening before the festival Juanita asked Brandon to take a stroll out on the beach before the sun went down completely. It was their routine walk to keep Brandon from becoming too stiff over time. Uncle Tony would usually join them except for this time he had laid down early. On the way back from their stroll Brandon spotted a familiar car parked on the side of the house. Just as they were about to step onto the patio, Carl, William and Leslie walked out to greet them with big smiles. "What are you two doing here so early? The festival isn't until tomorrow." Brandon asked while the two couples exchanges hugs with one another. "Do you want to tell them or can I tell them?" William asked Leslie. Leslie smiled and said "Be my guest." William pointed to the patio chairs suggesting that everyone take a seat and they did. He said "Well Leslie and I have something to tell you guys. We were not completely honest with you. We didn't actually stumble across Dolphin Manor like we told you." He reached into his back pocket then pulled out his wallet and passed them each a business card. "We are with the hit tv show 'Minding Your Manors' on HGTV." Immediately Juanita began squealing like a teenage girl. "Well I see that we have at least one fan." Leslie said to William. Juanita's loud shrieking sent Sydney running out to the patio asking "What's all the noise about?" Then right behind her came Uncle Tony moving in a slow steady pace. "What in the hell is going on out here with all of this ruckus?" he asked with a scowl. Carl stood to update Uncle Tony saying "Daddy you remember William and Leslie from awhile back when you were still in the hospital. They are from the TV show 'Minding Your Manors' on cable." He looked the two of them up and down and while taking a seat he said "Well they need to take their show's advice and mind their own manners and stop all of this shucking and jiving out here while folks is trying to sleep. Ya'll damn near scared the stitches out of me. And why is they here and not on TV?" Everyone fell out laughing at Uncle Tony except for Uncle Tony which was very much serious. "Well Mr. Patrick I'm glad you asked. We have a surprise for all of you. We would like to feature your bed and breakfast in our upcoming special. We have gone around to several and found yours to be the most interesting. Along with being featured we also extend our makeover crew at no cost to you. They will complete any renovations and repairs required. Your place has an amazing story that we feel our viewers will love; not to mention Leslie and I got engaged here and would like to also have our wedding here if you will allow it. So what do you say?" Uncle Tony turned around looking at everyone surrounding him. Carl asked "What are you looking at us for? You don't need our approval. Go ahead and tell the man yes." That's when Uncle Tony barked "Who in the hell told you I was looking for your approval. I was waiting to see if one of you were going to say no so I could slap a birth mark on you. Of course I say yeah. Who in the hell wouldn't?" Everyone including Uncle Tony all burst out laughing out loud.

Later that night after dinner Brandon asked Juanita to step out back with him. They walked out towards the shore and Juanita turn to Brandon and said "Now you know we have a big day tomorrow and have to get up early. You don't need to try and overdo it tonight. You'll need all of your energy for tomorrow." Brandon smiled and said "Listen I feel fine and I'm not going to be up much longer but it just feels so nice outside that I want to enjoy it for a moment." Juanita just smiled and tilted her head and nodded. They continued to walk on but instead of heading for the shore Brandon led them to the gazebo. "Let's have a seat here for a moment." Brandon suggested as he took a seat on one side of the swing. He brushed off the other side and held out his hand for her to sit next to him. When she was comfortably seated Brandon turned to her and said "Juanita we've known each other since we were both kids. And since I've come back to Silver Pointe, it seems as though we picked up where we left off. I have so many fond memories of my youth from both New York and North Carolina. For as far back as I can remember all of my most memorable ones involved you in some form or fashion. I can't think of anyone that makes me as happy as you. When I lost my wife I didn't think I would or even could love another woman again. And no sooner than I had it made up in my mind that I was going to have to accept the fact that I'm going to be single forever, God brought you right back into my life...and I thank Him for it." Juanita's eyes were beginning to water and a single tear rolled down her cheek. As hard as she tried, she could not help letting tears pour when she saw Brandon easing off of the swing to get on one knee before her. With a couple of quick grimaces he managed to upright himself. He reached in his pocket and looked her in the eyes and said "Juanita you have revived a side of me that I forgot I had. You have been the best thing that has happened to me in years. I feel as though we are on a roller coaster ride and I don't want it to ever stop. I allowed you to slip through my fingers many years ago without manning up. I will be damned if I will make that same mistake twice. Will you do me the honor of becoming my roller coaster co-pilot and be my wife?" Tears streamed down Juanita's face as she responded in a soft and shaky voice "Yes!" She extended her hand and allowed Brandon to place the ring on her finger. With a little help from Juanita he stood to his feet and planted a deep and passionate kiss on her lips. After several minutes of lip locking they tore themselves away from one another.

On their way back to the house Brandon glanced up to an upstairs bedroom window and caught Sydney and Uncle Tony spying on Juanita and him. He smiled and gave them the thumbs up to confirm that she said "Yes!" Sydney and Uncle Tony's cheers were muffled but loud enough to be heard outside. Just as they were about to walk through the door Juanita stopped Brandon and asked "There's something that I've been meaning to ask you... Just what WERE those pictures that you showed David the day he got arrested? And how did you get them?" Brandon laughed as he shook his head and said "Wow those pictures were the worst. I will show them to you but I have to warn you, David had a woman doing things to him with a cucumber that will make you see him in a whole different light. The fact that he was wearing some kind of tight, black leather

"Village People" outfit on made it even worse. But for the next seven to ten years in state lock up he is right where he will be able to get all of the man loving he needs." They laughed together and Leslie asked "So the only thing I don't get is why Trey and his father donated so much money!" Brandon smiled and said "Well years ago my grandfather loaned his grandfather money to open his store and among a few other things. Not once did he ask for any profit nor did he have any questions about what Mr. Watson was doing with the money. All he ever did was help a friend. So when I went to Trey he and his father gave us twenty thousand dollars along with the pictures and a letter explaining how it was in my grandfathers' honor. The festival and the party are going to be the talk of the town for a long time." Juanita wrapped her arms around Brandon then snuggled next to him and said "And with the television show coming, Silver Pointe is NOT going to be the same. See what you did? You came back to town and got my little hometown in an uproar. It must be that New York charm that I fell in love with years ago. It's gotten even stronger I see." She kissed his smiling lips and escorted him back into the house for a good night's rest for the festival in the morning.

Three months after a successful festival and after party for the high school reunion Dolphin Manor appeared on the season opening for Minding Your Manors. The episode was full of Uncle Tony antics that earned them record breaking ratings. The producers were so pleased with the response from their viewing audience that they paid Uncle Tony enough money to pay off the mortgage and put some away. The popularity from their television appearance increased their revenue by well over five times their best past year. The success of the manor also brought more tourists back to Silver Pointe which meant more money for the town as well. Meanwhile Brandon and Uncle Tony continued to heal and regain their strength. Brandon and Juanita had a small but elegant wedding under the gazebo at Dolphin Manor. Carl and Rusty were both Brandon's best men and Uncle Tony stepped up and gave Juanita to Brandon. Once strong enough to return back to New York, Brandon offered to move to North Carolina but Juanita refused to ask him to do that to Sydney. Although she knew that Sydney was willing and considering the move, Juanita also knew that Sydney would miss her friends she grew up with. It also was easier to take her practice to New York than it was for Brandon to try and prospect for new business. With Juanita graduating at the top of her class and completing a few courses early she had no doubt that she would quickly earn the privilege to practice in New York as well. So the three of them went to

New York and started a new life. On Thanksgiving and one week in the summer they go back to Silver Pointe to visit friends and family while David West sat in prison cursing the day that Brandon Patrick came to Silver Pointe.